Fight or Flight

Unbreakable, Volume 2

Hannah Martinez

Published by Hannah Martinez, 2023.

FIGHT OR FLIGHT

First edition. November 14, 2023.

Copyright © 2023 Hannah Martinez.

ISBN: 979-8223464211

Written by Hannah Martinez.

For my best friend of more than two decades. I couldn't have made it without you.

CHAPTER I

CLAIRE

I concentrate on my therapist's hand as she plays with her pen. *Click, click.*

"Claire?" I hear her annoying voice as if from a distance, when in reality, we're sitting almost face to face in her small office.

Click, click.

With each click, I have to fight the urge to rip it from her chubby little fingers.

"You seem agitated today," she says, and I direct my sight toward her cold, blue eyes.

I smile at her sweetly and relax back in the plushy armchair. "I'm not. What gave you that idea?"

She licks her lips, which are covered with remnants of crusty, red lipstick before she smiles at me knowingly as if we have more than a few secrets to share between us. As if we are friends.

"You just seem tense. Are you balancing your medication well?"

"I am," I lie simply and look back at her hand. *Click, click.*

"Well, then. I'm glad. So, why don't you tell me how your week is going so far?" She asks pleasantly and lifts her notepad that is lying in her lap as if to get ready to write a report.

I blink at her, my smile intact, but inside, I feel the liquid fire lick at my insides, basically asking me to attack her. The aggression spikes should be a pretty good indicator that I am on a straight path to cuckoo town, but I squish it down quickly.

"Haven't you watched the news, Ms. Edwards?" I ask with what, I hope, is a neutral tone.

She tilts her head to the side and writes something on the piece of paper as she questions, "What is it that you would like me to see there, Claire?"

For a second, I wonder, what exactly is she writing? It's probably some nonsense to make her look professional or some other bullshit. Well, she can't fool me. She's so bad at her job. Ms Edwards is way more concerned with trying to find a husband and flirting with my dad whenever he's picking me up than actually getting to know me, let alone help me.

As soon as I'm eighteen, which will be in four agonizing months, I'll be cutting my ties with that woman ASAP. My father won't be able to make me come see her anymore.

"Claire?" She prompts me to answer with her eyebrows furrowed in plain frustration.

I try to once again keep my anger at bay when I eventually reply. "My best friend had to run from her psycho dad. You know him. Your beloved sheriff David Wallace," I can't contain the sneer that comes over my face as I spit his name.

She makes an unpleasant face but keeps her voice soft. "Your friend, Jennifer, was always a very troubled young lady, Claire. From my understanding, no one knows what happened to her exactly. She was clearly a bad influence on you, and now she's a runaway. You know we are a small community here at Bell Ridge, and Sheriff Wallace..."

"Almost burned a fucking guy alive because he discovered what that piece of shit been up to!" I explode and grab onto the handrests just so I don't squeeze the life out of this useless creature that keeps staring at me in shock.

It was the first time when I showed so much emotion and animosity toward her, and I could see by the sharp intake of breath that she did not see that coming.

Before she can compose herself, I jump up from my seat and glance at the giant clock on the wall.

"I have to go to school. I'll see you next week, Ms. Edwards," I say hurriedly and grab my backpack from the floor.

"Claire, wait, we still have..." she scrambles from her seat, her face getting a little red.

I swing my bag on one shoulder and open the door to exit the office in haste, passing by my surprised father, who was sitting in the waiting area, reading some kind of sports magazine.

He jumps up from his seat when he sees me and opens his mouth to speak, but I just mutter, "I'll wait in the car while she tattles on me."

I STARE DISPASSIONATELY through the windshield of my father's car at the kids standing in front of the school, laughing together, talking about insignificant shit. Plotting to skip classes and planning the next party they will throw at the Mill.

It wasn't that long ago when Jenny and I were a part of it.

Where is she? Will she come back for me? Can I keep going without her presence calming me down?

My father clears his throat to get my attention and shifts uncomfortably behind the wheel. Sometimes, I feel sorry for the guy when I see his pathetic attempts at parenting.

He didn't sign up for a life with a crazy wife, so he ran as far as he could, leaving my mom to fend for herself. What he probably didn't expect was getting a younger supplement on his doorstep several years later.

I admit that I can see he cares, and he tried to get to know me at first, but instead of getting closer, we drifted further and further apart.

So, yeah, usually I feel sorry for him when I see him fidgeting like he is now.

But now I don't. Not after I told him about Jenny, and he didn't believe me. Not after I begged him to look for her after Brody got roasted in that warehouse by that monster. Not after I lost my only friend. The only light in my otherwise bleak reality.

"Claire... I worry about you. Your latest behavior has shown that your *disease* is getting worse," he licks his lips and glances at me quickly before looking ahead again. "Maybe we should call Doctor Starwood..."

"No," I say firmly, my voice colder than usual. "You know what we should do, though, *Dad*? We should stop making everything in my life about the disease, as you like to call it. Not everything I do or say is because of being fucking bipolar! I've got mood swings, I'm not retarded. But you're treating me like I'm incapable of making judgments or understanding reality. Does it get jumbled here sometimes?" I point to my forehead. "Yes, it does. But I'm still a person. My feelings are still valid. And what is happening in my life is fucking true. My friend is most probably in danger right as we're talking, and I can't do anything about it. And you'll be sitting there, along with Ms. Edwards, trying to convince me that it's all in my head!"

"Claire... I get that you are upset. But Sheriff Wallace and his wife are missing now, too. We don't know what happened there or if Jennifer was somehow involved in their disappearance..." he tries to convince me in a soothing tone, but I've had enough.

Before he can say another word, I grab my bag and open the passenger door.

"Yeah, sure, and I'm the delusional one here..." I throw sarcastically before I slam the door with enough force to shake the vehicle.

I'm literally fuming as I march toward the school entrance, slamming into whoever's in my way.

I knock into some guy, almost taking us both to the ground.

"Hey! Watch it, you freak!" He yells after me, but I don't even spare him a glance as I straighten myself and continue on my way even faster.

I walk into the girl's bathroom and lock myself in the stall, ignoring the bell announcing the start of the first period.

My mind is so messed up right now that I'm not even able to shed a tear. My arms shake as I try to get rid of the need to literally murder someone. The faces of people who let me down show in my mind on a constant loop.

I stopped taking my meds a couple of weeks ago, thinking I needed to maintain the sharpness of my mind with everything happening. But now I am starting to think that maybe it was a mistake. Jenny is not here to help me get through it all. There's nothing to outbalance the darkness that's been swallowing me whole, and it's been harder and harder to even see the way out of the dark plunge.

There's one way out of this.

No! No.

Jenny needs me. I promised her that I would wait. If she comes back... No. *When* she comes back, I will be here, ready to welcome her. She's probably somewhere close, just waiting for the dust to settle and for her father to get arrested so that she can come back safely.

She'll come back. I know it in my heart that I will see her again.

I'm almost calm when I hear the bell ringing after the end of the first class. Shit, I've been here longer than I thought. Oh, well, it's not like I care about school anymore. But, still, I better get to the second period.

I'm just thinking about that when I hear the doors to the bathroom open and a few vaguely familiar female voices carrying in.

"I don't believe that, Lisa. Marcus is just talking out of his ass because he's seeking attention..."

"Not this time. He was too smug about it..." the other girl replies, and I hold my breath, listening to the group of girls that, I thought, were my friends at some point.

"What do you think, Ella? Your dad was there, right? Maybe he mentioned something," the girl named Lisa asks.

There's silence for a few seconds, and I feel my whole body tensing because now I have a very good indication of what they are talking about.

Ella Diaz is the daughter of the police officer who supposedly saved Damon Brody's life. I never actually thought about speaking to her about it. I was too focused on the fact that Jenny was missing. Too focused on how it affects me.

"Well... My dad would kill me if he knew we're gossiping about it..." Ella sounds unsure, and I hear footsteps and some shuffling before the other voice pipes in.

"Don't be like that, El. For once, something interesting happens in Bell Ridge. I want to know all the juicy bits before the town goes asleep again," another excited voice pipes in.

"All right, fine. So... My dad is pretty much tight-lipped about the entire thing and gets angry whenever me or my mom ask about it. But I heard him talk to some detectives once, and he did mention a punk that played them into going to that warehouse. He didn't say it was Marcus, though, but it would line up with his story, I guess."

"I knew it! He was always so salty about that little skank dumping him! He said she was fucking that cop." Lisa laughs. "No wonder he's been in such a great mood lately..."

"I don't think it's funny, Lisa," Ella admonishes just as another bell rings out. "Come on. I can't be late again. We have a history test."

"Don't remind me. I swear Mrs. March wants to fail the whole..." The last voice gets cut off as they all exit the bathroom, with the door closing behind them with a loud click.

I stumble out of the stall and turn on the faucet to splash some cold water onto my face.

My breath is uneven, and I glance at my pale reflection. Do people really think that this is some kind of joke? A girl can be abused and treated like shit, and all they do is laugh? What kind of messed up world am I living in?

The yearning for someone to hold me and make it all go away grows to unbearable proportions. And yet again, I feel so lonely and helpless. I have no control. No control over my life, no control over my feelings, and no control over what's happening to the people I care about.

I stare into my own eyes for what feels like forever until my breath evens out, and I feel stable enough to leave the bathroom. I fluff my hair and pinch my cheeks to bring some color to them before grabbing my backpack and walking out.

CHAPTER II

BECAUSE IT'S LONG AFTER the next class started, I walk out in a rush not to get caught by a teacher when I decide to ditch the school altogether—too much emotion for one day. I won't be able to focus on anything useful anyway, at least not in a way that would make a difference to my already abominable grades.

My main focus on my escape; I don't pay attention to anything other than my shoes and end up bumping straight into someone. I almost tumble to the ground but am caught at the last second.

"Woah. Sorry, I didn't anticipate anyone being here. My bad." I hear a deep voice stating apologetically and look up at the guy that I've been kind of ogling from afar for the last few months.

Well, maybe not downright ogling, but I was intrigued ever since he started going to our school in the middle of last semester. There's something about him that makes me aware of his closeness whenever he's generous enough to grace the school with his presence. Kind of what I felt when I first laid my eyes on Jenny. Just some unexplainable connection on a primal level. Like, perhaps, he could be my friend.

I don't know his name since I was never even remotely close to voicing my interest or brave enough to ask around casually. I didn't even say anything to my best friend. She's been preoccupied with her father's outbursts. And also, the subject of men was a no-go zone after the drama with Marcus last year. So I felt stupid to even bring up my weird infatuation with a boy I don't even know.

But I've watched him. I people-watch quite a lot, and other students are already used to my staring. Not to say that they like it. Since I've been named the school weirdo almost since the beginning, no one cares, just assuming I'm retarded or something. Other than the occasional "What are you staring at, you freak?" No one pays me any mind anymore.

I don't know why exactly, but with this guy, I tried to be more subtle. And it's not like there were many opportunities I could do my secret scanning. He's barely attending school, from what I've seen, and I don't think he's in any of my classes. I'm not even sure if he's a junior or a senior. All I've gathered is that he's very good-looking – not that it's something that I care about; he's not from around here, and he's a loner.

He acts as if he doesn't have a care in the world around our peers, but I see through it. After all, playing the unbothered, happy person is my jam. Hiding the deep sadness and overall confusion about life behind the cheery exterior that isn't exactly fake. It's real, too—the most exhausting dichotomy to maintain in life.

He steps to the side and eyes the backpack hanging loosely from one of my shoulders before his eyes travel to my colorful shirt with a yawning sloth and then simply smiles. It's the first time in weeks since anyone directed a genuine smile in my direction, and I feel something stirring inside me. A new feeling that I have trouble naming.

"Ditching class?" He asks with humor sparking in his eyes.

My eyes widen at him, and I check behind me like an idiot, wanting to be sure it's actually me that he's addressing, and he chuckles.

"Um-uh, yeah… is that okay?" I have no idea why I feel the need to ask him for permission and want to facepalm immediately after the question leaves my mouth. If he hadn't heard about the school freak already, I'm sure now he's going to be able to figure out on his own who he's dealing with here.

One of his eyebrows lifts, but to my surprise, he doesn't mock me, just smirks slightly, trying to look conspicuous before he replies in a low voice, "I won't tell if you won't. I'm actually on the same mission right now."

"Really?" I question and eye the school entrance door with interest. "I wonder what you'll be doing after you get out of here," I voice my thoughts out loud, and then my eyes snap to his. Shit, Claire, stop asking strangers things that aren't any of your business.

Yet, the guy surprises me again when he just shrugs like it's normal, and we've been hanging out before. We start walking through the corridor. "Have to deal with some bullshit with my brother. Honestly, I would rather stay here, even though the chemistry class with Mrs. Berry is boring as shit, rather than deal with him. But what can you do, right? That's family for you."

He sounds a little bitter, but when I glance at him, his face appears relaxed.

"I'm Aidan, by the way," he says and opens the door for me.

"Claire," I reply as I move past him and tuck a strand of hair behind my ear self-consciously.

Just as we reach the last step outside, a truck pulls up in the school parking lot, and someone waves through the open window. Aidan lifts his hand in response and then peers down at me.

"Gotta go. Nice to meet you, Claire." There's nothing special about the way he's saying my name, but it still manages to make my heart beat faster somehow.

"Um, yeah. You too," I respond shyly and curse the blush that must be clear on my face with how hot my face feels.

I'm graced with a toothy smile before he starts walking away. Halfway to the truck, he stops and turns toward me as he continues retreating backwards.

"Hey, are you going to the Mill today, by any chance?"

"The Mill?" I repeat, completely stumped. No — is what I want to say immediately, but somehow, my head starts nodding before I know what's happening.

"Cool. See you there," he says and then jumps into the passenger seat of the waiting vehicle before it drives off with a squeal of tires.

Cool? No, not cool. What the hell?

WHAT AM I EVEN DOING here? I keep asking myself as I squeeze through the loud crowd of teenagers gathered around the huge bonfire. A heavy cloud of marijuana-scented smoke hits my nose, and I have to wave it away to see where I'm going.

I'm a little surprised that so much has changed in my life in the course of last month or last year even, but this place appears to be the same. Even some of the faces I recognize from the time Jenny, the group, and I hung around here every Friday night.

I've been changing my mind about coming ever since I agreed to meet Aidan here. Maybe I read too much into the whole situation? Was I actually invited? Is my mind playing tricks again? After all, he didn't say anything about going together. The entire interaction with him could be just in my head. I mean, I know it happened, but was there really interest in his eyes that I saw? Was his smile genuine, or did he mock me like all the other guys before him?

The problem is, I never know. But coming here even to be stood up felt like a better idea to spend the evening than sitting in my room alone and climbing the walls.

It's starting to get dark fast, but it's not hard for me to distinguish faces gathered around in small circles. After making two rounds around the place, I have to admit that there's no sign of Aidan anywhere, and it makes me feel like such an idiot.

My shoulders hunch when disappointment clouds my mind. I whirl around, set on coming back to town since it's not too late yet to walk on my own, only to come face to face with Jenny's evil ex, Marcus.

"Hey, I know you," he slurs, his posture unstable. "Didn't think Freaky Claire would ever grace this place without her Master Slut coming along. What is it, puppet, got lost on your own?"

I don't let him see how much his words anger me and just smile before walking around him. Then I recall what the girls in the bathroom said back at school and change my mind. Maybe he actually knows something of use.

"Actually, I wanted to talk to you?" I step back in front of him and throw him a daring look.

"Talking is not exactly up my alley when it comes to you," he laughs and then eyes me up and down in a predatory way. It makes me uncomfortable, but I try with everything I got to keep my brave face intact. He's drunk, and we're in a public place. There won't be a better moment to ask him about what happened.

"Come on," I grab his hand, trying not to wince at how clammy his skin is, and move a little further from the crowd, where it's a bit quieter, and we're hidden in a half-shadow.

"Well, well, I did not see that coming," he laughs and steps closer to me. I drop his hand as if it burned me and make a beeline when he tries to reach me, which isn't hard with how much alcohol he must have running through his veins right now.

"Playing hard to get?" Marcus asks angrily when I step away once again.

"Stop it. That's not why we're here, and you know it. I want to know what happened that day. With the cops? And... And with Jenny," my tone turns pleading at the end.

"She got what she deserved; that's what happened," he stumbles over his words. "If you're not gonna suck my dick, then I'm out of here."

"No, wait," I move around him and put a hand on his chest to stop him from getting away, which proves to be a mistake.

In the next second, he grabs my wrist and twists it painfully before pushing me away. The force makes me stumble, and I land on my butt in the overgrown, dried-up grass.

He bends over me and sneers in my face, "Don't mess with me, little girl, or I'll get rid of you just as I did with..."

"Hey! What the fuck are you doing?" A voice calls before Marcus is being pushed away from me, and I lift my head up to find Aidan glaring at the other man.

"Mind your own fucking business..." Marcus snarls but then suddenly takes a step back, his eyes widening. "Oh, shit, man. My bad. I didn't know it was you."

"I asked what the fuck are you doing?" Aidan repeats in a low voice and steps closer.

"We were just..." Markus starts unevenly, his eyes panicked and moving to me as if asking for help.

I ignore him and grab Aidan's offered hand to stand up, the worried look on his face melting my fear a bit.

I swallow the thoughts of what could've happened if he hadn't come to my rescue and smile wobbly. "It's fine. We had a misunderstanding."

"A misunderstanding?" Aidan's eyes go to Marcus, who nods his head rapidly. Not so tough now in the presence of someone bigger.

"Uh, yeah, man. I..." Marcus scratches at his neck and then looks back toward the crowd. I follow his line of sight and frown at the group of men standing on the side, all wearing a jacket with some kind of twirly gang symbol. Actually, now, come to think of it, I realize Aidan is wearing it, too.

"We're cool, right?" Marcus asks, and Aidan smiles coldly in response.

"Yeah," he mutters and then jerks his head to the side, motioning for Marcus to leave, to which he sighs in relief and almost runs away, checking over his shoulder twice to see if he's really in the clear.

"Welp, that escalated quickly," I comment and eye my rescuer with interest.

He rakes his fingers through his hair and huffs before gazing into my eyes with a furrowed brow.

"Are you okay? Now that he's gone, you can tell me if-"

"I'm really fine. My hand hurts a bit from where he grabbed me," I reply. Aidan's face twists, and he looks in the direction where Marcus disappeared as if ready to go after him, so I quickly tug on his jacket to get his attention. "But honestly, I'm fine. He's not worth the hustle, you know?"

"Hmm, yeah," he nods absentmindedly, still not looking at me.

I tug once again before letting go, and he finally looks back at me.

"Thank you. For you know... Stepping in when you did," I shuffle my legs a bit, not knowing what to say. I'm scared; one wrong word from me, and the guy will run for the hills.

"Yeah, sorry I didn't reach you before it came to that. I was looking for you at the house and then by the fire. When I didn't see you anywhere, I assumed you didn't come but then thought I saw you..."

Does he actually look a bit flustered, or am I imagining it? He was just playing Mr. Tough Guy a second ago, and now he looks all shy and uncertain. A grin overtakes my face.

"You were looking for me?" I put a hand on my chest, where I feel my heart flutter giddily.

"Um, yeah? I mean, we talked today at school?" He bites the inside of his cheek and then raises his hands up. "I mean, if it was not what you-"

"It was. It totally was," I cut in and am immediately gifted with a relieved smile.

"Oh. So, do you want a drink or something? Or maybe we can just sit and talk?" He waves around, acting just as awkward as I would normally do.

He's so different from the cool guy that I met at school this morning. Or even the bad boy ready to throw fists a few minutes ago. I don't know which version I like better. But this Aidan feels the most relatable. Usually, I am the one who has trouble approaching new people. It's a relief to see someone else struggle for once.

"Sure," I reply in a chirping voice and motion toward the empty beer crates that someone before us positioned upside down to create makeshift seats.

The sun is almost fully down, so it takes a moment for my eyes to adjust and see his face, but when I do, I'm surprised to discover a deep frown marring his face.

"What's wrong?"

"Nothing, it's just that... I was a bit surprised to see you walking away with Marcus. He's not exactly the type of guy I would think a pretty girl like you would socialize with. I mean, why would you wander away with him?" There's no accusation in his voice, just concern, but all I am able to focus on is what he said about me.

"You think I'm pretty?" My voice is timid.

He hesitates before looking straight at me. "I do."

"I think you're pretty, too. I mean, not pretty. That's too feminine, right? So, let me rephrase that. Whenever I watched you at school, I thought you were really handsome. Uh, not that I was watching you. I mean, not in a creepy way. Because I was watching you. But again, not in a creepy way. Just interested in who you are and what you're doing."

I watch amusement appear on his face as he tilts his head to the side as if trying to analyze me to see if I'm joking.

"So, I was also wondering why did you ask me to come to the Mill. Because you did ask me, right? I mean, you just confirmed that you did. But you're you, and you're cool and obviously came with a group of friends, so it's not like you're an actual loner like I assumed at school."

"Uh-huh?" He blinks at me, now looking slightly confused, which makes me fidget because I know my stupid mouth is ruining this.

"I just mean... Um. I wonder why would you be interested more in sitting here with me when I'm obviously not more fun than dancing with your friends and getting drunk or whatever it is that you like to do."

"Do you wonder about things often?"

"Yep," I reply. "And I talk a lot, too."

"You don't say..." he says with a chuckle.

I look to the side and sigh. "You're making fun of me."

Aidan nudges my leg with his knee and convinces, "I'm not."

I roll my eyes but don't reply.

"To answer your question. Yes, I came here with other people. Friends? Not exactly. I'm here with my brother and our... group. But since I'm not really into those kinds of things, I was already trying to split when I didn't see you anywhere..." he trails off. "Anyway, um, I've seen you at school before today too. And I kind of found you intriguing. So, you can say we've both been watching each other. Of course, not in a creepy way."

The playful smile he shoots my way makes me slightly lightheaded, and I can't help but lean closer to him. I notice the way he eyes my lips before looking up.

"You find me intriguing?" I ask slowly, tasting the word. "I've been called many things in my life, but never that."

"What other things people have called you?"

"Oh, the list is too long, but nutjob and loony tunes have been the top two this week," I say matter-of-factly.

"And you're okay with this?" He looks angry on my behalf, and I immediately want to take it back. This is not the direction I want our conversation to go. I've learned already not to tell people that I have mental health issues. It's better if they think I'm just strange or even a freak.

When you've got that stuff on paper, it changes how people act around you.

"They're not wrong. I am... different. And I've faced some, um, problems. When my friend Jenny was here, she fought everyone who even looked badly my way. She needn't have to, to be honest. As long as she was with me, I didn't care about other people and what their feelings about me were. But she wouldn't have it, no," I say wistfully and feel as if an invisible knife just stabbed me in the heart at the fresh reminder of her being gone.

"So where is she?" Aidan asks, almost as if he's scared of the answer.

"Heard about the sheriff thing?"

"Um, yeah. It's fucking Bell Ridge. Of course, I've heard," he replies, his voice turning a little harsh.

I blink at him. "And you heard about his daughter?"

He scratches his head and looks away. "Yeah," but then snaps his head to look at me from under lowered eyebrows. "Wait. You don't mean..."

"That's Jenny—my best friend. I'm surprised you didn't hear about it. With all the rumors floating around this last month."

Aidan blinks twice and swallows. "I've been keeping to myself lately. I didn't go around much, so no... I don't know what the rumors are. And, uh. I'm... I'm sorry." I give him a confused look, and he clarifies, "About your friend. I hope she'll be found safe and sound soon."

I hum in my throat but don't answer.

"So was the argument with that asshole Marcus about that? I thought I heard somewhere that he used to date the sheriff's daughter. That's if... If you don't mind me asking," Aidan asks quietly, looking straight ahead.

"You can say that they used to... um, you know. And I think he maybe knows more about what happened after she ran away than he lets on."

"Like... about the thing with the FBI agent and the warehouse getting burned out?"

"Yeah," I reply, feeling the cold anger spike in me again.

I look up in surprise when suddenly Aidan gets up and then pulls me by my arm to go with him.

"Come on, I'll give you a ride home. It's late, and I can't let you stay here alone," he says, his voice sounding almost robotic, and he's not meeting my gaze.

Did I say something to upset him?

CHAPTER III

I STAND TO THE SIDE and observe his interaction with his brother, who looks like the opposite of Aidan. Where he is tall and lean, with thick black hair and a barely-there stubble, his brother is short, bulky, with a shaved head and a goatee. The brother's neck is covered with colorful designs that reach the back of his skull, adding to his already menacing look.

The group of men that stand around them all look similar to Baldy over there. Muscled and dangerously looking.

They laugh mockingly when Aidan's brother says something, and I don't like how they are looking at him. I'm a little too familiar with that look. Like, what you're saying is not valid. Like you're the one odd out. And like you're not in on the joke; instead, you *are* the joke.

I swing my eyes back to Aidan when the brothers start to fight, their raised voices carrying over the field and causing a few heads to turn toward them. He looks seriously pissed off, and I gulp. I'm not sure if it's caused by the better light illuminating his features and making him stand out among the other men. Or if it's the angry, macho stance he now has with the furrowed brow and glaring eyes, but I'm even more attracted to him all of a sudden. As in interested in something else than just his personality or his heart. Wow. That's new for me.

My eyes drink him in as a fire of desire spreads from my core, heating my body, which was mostly numb until that point. I never felt that kind of pull toward someone, and even went so far as to claim that maybe I'm asexual or that there's something wrong with me.

Now, how can I get him to feel the same pull toward me? Does he find me attractive? I know he said I'm intriguing. But really, what does that mean in his world?

Jenny would probably say something like, "Just be yourself, Claire. And if he doesn't like it, then he can fuck off."

Aidan finishes bickering with the group of men standing around the fire and then, with a shake of his head, walks toward me and grabs me by the shoulders to stir me away. Wow, it feels good to be enveloped like that by his heavy arm.

The men yell something behind us that I don't quite catch, and Aidan lifts a middle finger above his head with a muttered, "Assholes."

He looks troubled, but the thrill that runs through me at his touch keeps me quiet for a bit as we walk to the edge of the woods.

When we're past the line of people still mulling around, Aidan drops his arm to get his phone out to turn on the flashlight.

"My brother wouldn't let me borrow his truck, so we'll have to walk, if that's okay with you." He says with a clenched jaw, and I hope he's not angry that he will have to spend some more time with me.

"I love walking," I gush enthusiastically and step at his side.

"All right, let's go then," he replies and grabs my hand, presumably so I don't trip on anything, but I swear I already hear church bells resonating in my messed-up head.

By the way, I sigh, you could think he's just proposed to me. I was never good at keeping away from people that I felt drawn to. I just hope this one will not turn out to be a disaster.

"You don't get along well with your brother?" I hear myself asking when we step on the path that is a known shortcut to the country road leading toward Bell Ridge.

"Most times, we manage not to tear each other's heads off, but lately, things have been... tense. We had a disagreement of sorts, and ever since, Saint acts like the world's biggest asshole. Still, he's all I've got, so..." He drops my hand to move a branch to the side so that I can step ahead of him.

I almost snort at the fact that his brother's name is Saint, but somehow manage to school my features. "You don't look like brothers," I observe instead.

"We have different fathers. What about you, do you have siblings?"

I know I shouldn't feel so giddy about the fact that he seems genuinely interested, but the constant attention and validation seeker in me rears its ugly head immediately.

"Oh, no. At least, not that I know of. I would love to, though. Mom and I used to live in an isolated house amid the woods with my grandpa. I'm from a small village in Alaska. So, growing up, I always dreamt about having more people around me to play or talk to, you know? Mostly, I talked to the animals and plants... Shit, that's probably super weird."

He chuckles into the surrounding darkness before helping me step over a fallen log. "I don't think it's weird. We all need company. Someone to talk to. People aren't exactly made to be solitary creatures."

"And who do you talk to, Aidan?" I can't help but ask, detecting the underlying sadness in his voice.

He's quiet for a while, and I wonder if I didn't step over some invisible boundary.

But then he says, "Also myself, I guess. Which makes me sound like such a loser."

"So you're saying that I'm a loser because I used to speak to myself?" I tease, not really offended.

He makes big eyes at me, the light from the flashlight making them glow. "No. No. Of course not. This is not what I meant. Just that... Ah, shit. I'm not making a very good impression, am I?"

"Are you trying to make one?" I smile, my heart starting to beat wildly. Oh my God, maybe he does like me.

Aidan laughs nervously. "Yeah, maybe. How am I doing?"

"I would say pretty well. You stopped Marcus from... whatever he was going to do to me, and now you're walking me home, even though it's a bit of a long trip. You could've just stayed and enjoyed the rest of your night or maybe found better company. But I'll let the loser comment slide if you'll admit that the fact that you're lonely doesn't make you a loser."

"Okay. Deal," he chuckles lightly. "So, Alaska, huh? When did you move to Bell Ridge?"

We make it to the road, illuminated by the moonlight, and Aidan hides his phone and again takes my hand, even though it's not necessary anymore. The feel of his warm palm against my colder one makes me smile happily before I remember I was asked a question.

I lift my head to find him watching me with interest. "I moved here a few years back. I had to come here to live with my dad. Which is kind of a bummer."

"You don't like it here?"

"I love it, actually. Bell Ridge is way more interesting. There are people all around to observe, and I was able to find my best friend here. And sometimes even school is fun. Of course, now everything is like shit, and I feel murderous at times because the good times were taken away. But I still have hope that it will all be resolved soon."

Aidan hums in his throat, looking grim for a second before he snaps out of it. "I moved here about a year ago, and interesting isn't exactly the word I would use to describe this place."

"You sound just like Jenny. Or probably like most of the teenage population that lives here. Everyone seems to be just waiting to get out of here..."

"You don't?"

"Not at this particular moment, no," I smile at him coyly, to which he smirks, and we continue on our way for a few minutes in comfortable silence.

"You said your brother is all you've got. What about your parents, if you don't mind me asking?"

"Oh. Um. I never knew my father, and my mother is... not around. I've been staying with Saint for a few years. We lived all over the place since then, traveling as a group. Usually, we don't stay for longer at one place. Bell Ridge is the longest stop we had, to be honest. And to my dismay, it doesn't seem like we'll be out of here anytime soon."

"So, it's all horrible for you here?" I question, and he stops me.

I'm not exactly sure what the look on his face means, yet again, this slight shiver of heated anticipation takes root in my body. He bites his lip before stepping closer—no space left between us.

"Actually, I am just now discovering that it's not all so awful. Bell Ridge appears to have at least one thing that the other places I lived at were missing."

"Like what?" I ask and then gasp soundlessly when Aidan leans toward my face like he's going to kiss me. At the last moment, he shifts and goes straight to my ear.

The hand that's not holding mine currently moves to my cheek, and my eyes flutter shut at the gentle touch.

"This pretty, intriguing girl that I just met. I honestly was pretty nervous about the thought of approaching her before. So imagine what I felt when she fell right into my arms at school. Like it was meant to be," he whispers.

I sense his breath on my ear and gulp when a new, more intense sensation enters my core. It's hot like lava, and I have to stop myself from moving my legs to ease the newly awakened tension between my thighs.

He leaves a small kiss right under my earlobe, and I have to bite my lip. I've never even kissed a boy before today, so even this little, subtle touch has me almost melting on the spot. I've never felt like this before.

I'm so disappointed when he moves away and starts walking again that I almost scream at him to kiss me. I want him. So bad. And I was never good at keeping myself from people that I wanted. Or contain my instincts. That's just not me.

So, I allow him to lead me toward the illuminated town in the distance while we talk about things that don't really register. My mind is too scrambled, already running a mile a minute, thinking of a way to get what I want. To possess Aidan in every way possible and to make him mine.

CHAPTER IV

AIDAN

It makes my blood boil whenever my mind goes back to the image of that weasel Marcus putting his disgusting hands on Claire and pushing. If he thinks he's off the hook after that stunt, he's got a surprise coming. I just didn't want to make a scene in front of Claire, seeing as she's already had enough bad experiences for one evening.

What I've said about noticing her before is true. Many times, I found myself looking for her in the crowd, even though I had no idea who she was. But with everything happening right now, I know I shouldn't even look for a girlfriend or anything like that. And one look at her tells me casual wouldn't be enough with her. She's worth more than that.

Asking Claire to the Mill was more of a spur-of-the-moment thing that I didn't have time to think through, and I told myself we'd just hang around and maybe talk, and this is all whatever. Yet, I still felt a heavy pang of disappointment when I didn't find her anywhere when I got to the place.

And was even more disappointed when I saw her dragging Marcus away. I was honestly surprised by how much the image angered me on the spot like I had claimed the girl already when, in reality, it was just today that I learned her name.

I almost turned away, but then I saw her body language, and she looked more than uncomfortable, which made me pause and observe. And then react.

Going to the old farm was the last thing on my agenda for today when I woke up. All I wanted to do was to close myself in my room, surrounded by some heavy sounds and a few sheets of paper getting filled with my drawings.

Lately, that's all I've been feeling like doing. Submerging myself in my art is the only outlet I find soothing for the guilt that's been crashing me with each day. The deep disappointment and disgust for myself that I have to carry like a heavy backpack strapped to my back as I try to climb higher.

But of course, since the gang was going, I couldn't say no.

My brother Santiago, who's ironically being called the Saint by the rest of the guys, decided it's time to get back out in the open since he felt like "the dust has settled enough". I couldn't disagree more. Which I did, as well as repeated my ongoing concern about the moronic decision to stay in Bell Ridge after everything.

At this point, we're like sitting ducks.

But Saint won't ever listen to me. He got away with too much shit within his "career" and is getting cocky. He thinks he's invincible and nothing can touch him.

Well, I hope he's right. We may have our differences, and I hate the life that he condemned me to, but he's still my brother. The only person who ever cared for me enough to take me in.

Until I was twelve years old, I kept bouncing around different family members. My mother often left me for what meant to be just a few days, only to be gone for months, until she disappeared completely one day after a quick phone call to my grandma stating that "motherhood just ain't for her".

I wasn't surprised. Just terrified of the vision of going to live with some strangers after my grandmother decided that I was too much of an inconvenience.

It's when Santiago showed up. Up to that time, he was a stranger to me. A much older brother whom I had never seen before that day. My mother abandoned him when he was just a baby, leaving him with his father.

Living with Saint and the *Culebras* gang wasn't a fairy tale in any sense of the word, but I always got food on the table, a place to sleep, and a promise of a brotherhood that would stand by me no matter what.

At twelve, I was mesmerized, not having any idea what being in a gang could actually mean. I just saw the constant partying, doing whatever you want without any regard for other people outside the group, and getting easy money all the time.

I thought it was fucking cool, and I couldn't wait until I turned sixteen to be claimed as a full member. The tattoo of the snake curling around the bloody dagger was something I honestly dreamt of.

How fucking stupid I was.

Talking about stupid. How stupid is it of me to know I definitely shouldn't be doing something, yet here I am doing it. This is like a recurring theme in my life.

I should undoubtedly stay away from Claire and keep pushing Saint to leave Bell Ridge. But what do I do? Instead, insinuate myself even more into this new thing with her, wanting to know everything there is to know about her quirks.

I can't explain why am I still here and not running the other way. I know what I'm trying to do is the peak of my dumbness and can only lead to something dangerous. But the pull is just too strong.

It scares me. No girl other than Claire had this effect on me before. Not one.

Now, I glance at her as she marches on next to me, with her features only illuminated by the faint stream of light coming from the streetlight two blocks down. Long blond hair sways in the wind around her, making her look like a beautiful phantom. Her big eyes move from side to side as she drinks everything in as if she sees it for the first time.

And I can feel a new kind of fascination growing in me. My hands itch to draw her features. To freeze each expression on her face for long enough to let me immortalize her unusual, clear beauty on paper.

Other than her obvious hotness, I'm really drawn to her as a person. The way she views the world seems both childish yet mature, like she possesses some kind of wisdom that the rest of the people don't have access to, including myself.

Perhaps I am exaggerating. Maybe what Claire claims people say about her is true, and she has a screw loose somewhere in that pretty head of hers.

Or maybe I'm seeing it just right, and those people are just too stupid and ignorant to see the real value of having people like her around.

When we are close to my street, I don't break the silence. Just continue to walk toward my house. Claire doesn't protest, so I assume she has to live in the same area as me. That is until we reach the yard cluttered with motorcycle parts and empty bottles and stop.

"How far from here is your place?" I ask, and Claire stops before turning to me with a faraway look.

"Hm? Oh, not far..." Then she points toward my place with raised eyebrows. "Is this your house? I would love to see it."

"Oh. Sure," I scratch at my head. I didn't plan on asking her to come in.

I was thinking about giving her a small goodbye kiss on her doorstep and maybe asking her out on a date. The thought of us being alone right now in an enclosed space excites me, but still, I don't want to assume we will be doing anything. However, I am just a horny guy, so of course, it's not so easy to battle the inappropriate thoughts as they assault my mind.

I have to literally shake my head at the vivid images that make me blush slightly as I let Claire into the house.

She reads my expression incorrectly, and her face softens a little as she grabs onto my arm and squeezes.

"You don't have to be embarrassed, Aidan. I don't care about the material things or money."

"Uh. What?" I blink at her and just now realize how the house I share with Saint must look to someone from the outside.

I'm so used to the garbage way of living I share with the other men that I didn't even think of that factor.

I glance at the ugly yellow wallpaper in the corridor and the dirty carpet with burnt holes from cigarettes being stomped on it. Then I look into the kitchen and see the mismatched chairs and dirty old pots thrown into the moldy sink. I have to refrain from visibly cringing.

Shit, I live in a dump. I was so excited that Claire invited herself in that I didn't even think about the state the house is in. Now, my face gets even more red than before, and I wish I just walked her home.

But it's already too late.

"So, do you have a room or... ?" Claire questions, turning to me. She either really doesn't care about my house, or she's really good at hiding her initial reactions.

"Yeah, come on," I reply with relief.

My room is actually the nicest area in the house. Also, the cleanest. Mainly because I don't allow the gang members or anyone else to come in.

Claire walks ahead of me, and I try not to wince at the state I left it in. I've been getting a little crazy with my sketches lately, and on every surface available, there's paper covered in dark swirls. Some drawings are wrinkled and only half-finished; some already done. All of them are black and disturbing.

"Sorry about the mess," I mutter as I take a fast sweep around my room. "Would you like something to drink?"

"Sure. Whatever you have is fine," she mutters distractedly, already eyeing the obsidian, disfigured face of a monster trying to crawl its way out of a mirror.

"That's incredible," she gushes before grabbing the next one from my desk.

"I'll go grab the drinks," I say and quickly retreat from my bedroom.

I'm not angry at Claire for looking at my drawings, but I'm not used to sharing that part of me with anyone. My brother used to mock me about it, so I started to hide whatever came from my hand.

I quickly grab two cans of soda from the fridge and do a mental pep talk on my way back to start behaving like a normal human around Claire, or otherwise, I'm going to blow it.

I'm stopped in my tracks when I enter the room and see her standing in the middle of the room facing me. Without a word, she drops her jacket and lifts her shirt to let it fall behind her, revealing a black lacy bra on a set of perky breasts.

Swallowing heavily, I drag my gaze from her perked nipples, which are on full display through the translucent fabric, and look at her in question.

My dick stands up in full attention, but I ignore it completely as I rasp out, "Claire, what are you doing?"

Without hesitation, she opens the fly of her jeans and, in one swift motion, drags them down her incredible, shapely legs to then step out of them with a kick that sends them back.

"Everyone says that sex makes them feel good. I want to feel good for once, Aidan," she says confidently and blinks her big eyes at me.

Trying to think of a way to respond to that, I make the mistake of taking a full look at her standing there in just her underwear. When my eyes stop on her simple black panties, I notice the way her belly shifts in a sudden intake of breath, and I almost drop the soda cans, finding it hard to stop myself from reaching out to touch her.

I move closer to the bedside table and place our drinks there before giving her my full attention again.

"Claire... You know we don't have to... That's not why..." My mouth turns dry, and I don't know what I'm even trying to say here.

I don't know why I'm feeling so torn right now. Here is this beautiful, almost naked girl standing in my bedroom, basically asking me to fuck her. I should be halfway through getting myself out of my own clothes. Normally, that would be the case.

But there's just something about Claire. I have this tugging feeling that she needs more, and one thing I know for sure is that she's definitely too good for a scum like me. I can somehow attest to the pureness of her heart, even if I've known her for a day.

Yet, at this moment, there's nothing left of the babbling girl from before, appearing to be unsure of herself. She still looks sweet and small. But there's no vulnerability in her gaze or even a shadow of doubt. She looks completely calm as she steps closer to me to put her hand above my heart. Her head barely reaches my chin, and I feel her soft hair tickling the skin on my neck before she asks quietly.

"Will you make me feel good, Aidan?"

"Why me?" I whisper back stupidly, still fighting with myself to not reciprocate her touch.

She tilts her head back and, looking at my lips, replies, "There's just something about you. I don't know what it is, but I think you get me. The real me and that's so *intriguing*."

My heartbeat speeds up as she starts to caress my torso with her fingers, almost like she would play some kind of instrument.

"Do you want me?" She questions, her gaze colliding with my own, her pupils dilating slightly, making her eyes look almost obsidian.

"Yes," I reply honestly, my hand lifting on its own accord to touch the soft skin on her arm.

It's then that she stands on her tippy-toes to reach my lips and comes so close that I can almost taste her minty breath on my tongue.

I don't know who closes the last remnants of distance between us. Before I know it, our lips touch, and I'm gone.

My hands go everywhere, relishing in the feel of her small yet feminine curves. My tongue slips into her open mouth, making me yearn for more. Without moving away, I slip out of my leather jacket and start to back her away slowly toward the bed.

She matches my enthusiasm fully. Kiss for kiss, touch for touch. Claire moans loudly when my hand lands on her breast.

Hastily, she starts tugging on my shirt, so quickly I take it off and groan when she starts kissing my pecs, with her nails slowly dragging downward to reach into my pants.

Unable to wait any longer, I lower her onto the mattress and kneel between her open thighs.

Jesus Christ, if I had known that this would be how this evening would end up, I would never have fought my brother so much about going to the Mill today. And if I hadn't been there to see that dipshit's hands on my girl...

I snap my eyes to her face and am met with a fiery, daring look.

My girl? I've known Claire for like two seconds, and I'm already putting a claim on her. What the hell, dude…

My thoughts get immediately scrambled into nothingness when Claire uses the small moment of hesitation to her advantage. She sits up slightly and unclasps her bra, giving me an unobscured view of her beautiful tits.

If it's possible, my cock swells even more in my jeans, making it almost painful.

Working on an instinct, I lean in and lick the puckered nipple before going to the other, satisfied when I get a surprised squeak from Claire that turns into a low moan as I twirl my tongue around the hard bud.

She raises her hand blindly, searching for the opening of my fly and gasps when I slip one finger into her panties and tease her on her most intimate parts.

I get her worked up as she fumbles with the zipper and then curse loudly when her hand closes over my dick.

"Aidan?" She asks, her voice sounding unsure for the first time, and I stop what I'm doing to give her my full attention.

"Do you want me to stop?" I ask, sounding winded.

"No!" She exclaims forcefully and stops my hand from retreating, and I lift my eyebrows in question. She licks her lips and glances at the bulge in my pants.

"It's just that I have never done this before. Sure, I watched lots of porn out of curiosity and stuff, but it's not the same…"

A sound escapes from my throat, something between a groan and amusement, but she ignores me.

"... as actually doing it. So, I want you to teach me how to do it so it feels good to you."

"Claire, maybe we should stop. I don't want you to feel obliged..." I start, not fully believing that I'm actually trying to say no to a girl like Claire, that's currently lying under me in my bed with a hand on my dick. But it's my last resort to not think of myself as a total bastard.

"Can you please shut up already? We both know you're not some knight in shining armor rescuing a damsel in distress here. You want to fuck me, and I want to get fucked by you. The only thing standing in the way is my lack of experience and some dumbass chivalrous thing you are trying to do. I want my first time to be with you, Aidan. This is my choice. I picked you. If you don't want that, you can tell me to fuck off, but otherwise just get on with..."

I don't let her finish as my mouth lands on her with renewed passion, and I finally let go of all of my restrictions.

I get us both fully naked and am grabbing for a condom from my bedside drawer in no time.

Positioning myself at her entrance, I look up one last time into her eyes and mutter, "There will be no going back."

"Good," she whispers before I slowly slide into her.

At this moment, it is everything. Pure bliss. A connection like I never knew before.

And even at this time, I know, though I can't fully explain it yet, that something life-changing is happening to me. A part of my heart shifts, attuning itself to Claire's.

In the back of my mind, I know I'll have to pay for it someday. Probably sooner than later.

CHAPTER V

CLAIRE

I've been walking on cloud nine ever since I met Aidan. I'm so happy that I could scream from the rooftops about how he makes me feel.

Even my therapist noticed my improved behavior and praised me for making progress. Of course, I didn't share the reason for my good mood with her. If I could, I would keep what's between me and Aidan hidden from the world forever.

Yes, I still worry about Jenny. And keep an ear out for any rumors regarding the sheriff or his missing daughter, but I won't lie and say that my new relationship with Aidan didn't push everything else into the background.

I'm completely obsessed with him and love to observe him when he thinks I'm not looking.

We've been sneaking around for three weeks. Yes, Aidan picks me up after school where everyone can see us, and we hang around at his house until it's my time to come back home to my waiting, frowning father. What my dad doesn't know, though, is that most nights, I sneak out as soon as the light in his bedroom turns off, going straight back to Aidan's.

The way he awakens my body is just out of this world, and every time I think about something new that we did, my body grows hot. I'm becoming addicted to his loving touch, the soft words of praise, and the little noises he makes when I bring him pleasure.

Whenever he thinks I'm asleep, he turns on the little light and goes on to work on his art. Yes, I've seen it the day we met, but after that, they always stay hidden. I'm curious about it, but so far, he's been too shy about it. Every time I bring it up, he clams up. Saying that he's not ready to share it yet. I get it, but at the same time, it makes me sad that he doesn't trust me yet, as if I would ever laugh at him or criticize anything he does. The man is perfection.

He tries to act tough and manly around his brother and his idiotic friends, but as soon as the door closes, keeping us safe from the world outside, he shows me his soft side. Aidan can be thoughtful, caring, and gentle. He can also goof around like no other, and I love it.

I think I love him.

Yet, there's something indistinguishable between us—this intangible worry. Sometimes, I will catch him staring at me with a dose of fear or sadness. Sometimes, he smothers me with his affection, like he's scared I'll disappear or lose interest.

Which seems laughable to me. Because now, I can't imagine a day without seeing Aidan. Touching Aidan, showing love to Aidan.

He's all I can think about, and there is a small, tiny part of me that acknowledges that people would probably say it's not healthy. Well, they can suck it because I don't think I have ever been happier. I didn't have a depressive episode since our paths crossed. And my anger outbursts are nonexistent.

So, maybe people just have the wrong idea of what's healthy and what's not.

As soon as I walk outside of school with a giant grin on my face, ready to meet the source of my happiness, I take a look around the parking lot.

For two weeks now, Aidan was waiting close to the parking lot, ready to give me a ride home or take me to his place. He's barely attending school, busy with whatever Saint tells him to do, but he's always sure to make it in time to pick me up. Today, however, I don't notice him, and a pang of disappointment hits me like a sledgehammer. My grin transforms into a frown, and I step forward to search for Saint's truck.

I wait for five minutes. Then I wait for ten minutes. When it's apparent that he's not going to show up, my heart crumbles, and I have to stop the ongoing tears.

Then I roll my eyes and take out my phone. Can't be so dramatic and needy to cry the first time Aidan is late. Maybe something happened.

I click on his contact details and send him a message.

Forgot about me? ;)

Better play it off as nothing, so he doesn't know how much I'm already overreacting. I keep the phone in my hand and glance at the screen almost every second, hoping to see the reply, but almost break under the weight of dismay when, with each step, nothing happens.

I'm such a stupid girl. He's probably bored with me already. A guy like Aidan could have a different girlfriend each week.

I'm almost reaching my house when suddenly a familiar car is ahead. I follow it with my eyes and raise my eyebrows when it does a U-turn before stopping right where I stand on the sidewalk.

The passenger window lowers, and a sheepish-looking Aidan looks at me from behind the steering wheel.

All the negative emotions instantly leave my body when I basically skip toward the vehicle.

"Hi, stranger," I say with a flirtatious smile. "What brings you here?"

His mouth pulls up in a smirk, and he tilts his head to the side. "I just saw this beautiful girl walking all on her own, and I thought: my God, how is it possible that somebody didn't snatch her up already? Thought I'd make a move then."

"Really?" I laugh and get in.

As soon as I'm in the passenger seat, Aidan kisses me hard like he's a starved man and then releases me, only to caress my face with a troubled look.

"Sorry, I'm late, baby. There was this thing that I had to do for the *Culebras*. I was already on my way to get you, but Saint had me run another errand for him. The plus side is that he let me borrow his car without bitching so much. Again, I'm sorry."

"Psh," I flick my hand, trying to play it cool as if I weren't just full-on spiraling out of control because I've been on my own for five minutes. "It's fine. I thought something important must've kept you."

"Yeah," Aidan rubs at his neck and looks to the side.

I already asked him a few times what it is that they are doing, but so far, he's been tight-lipped. I pressed him one time, and he behaved like a caged animal, so I decided to just stop asking. Maybe it's not important. Or maybe I don't even want to know. I'm not stupid; I know they're in a gang, so it's probably illegal stuff. But I learned that I'm pretty good at ignoring the little red flags that Aidan has. I see it all; I just choose not to acknowledge it, worried that it will ruin what we have.

As soon as his eyes meet mine with a smile, I forget all about it.

"Do you have to come home, or can I take you somewhere?" He asks, and before he even finishes the question, I'm already nodding my head yes.

"Where are you taking me?" I ask, snapping the seat belt eagerly.

He laughs, looking at me like I'm truly precious before pulling onto the road again. "I have a surprise for you."

"Oh, my god, I love surprises," I squeal and tap my legs on the floor excitedly.

"And I love it when I can make you happy."

And I love you. I want to say, but won't dare to voice my feelings yet.

We drive out of town for a while, submerged in a comfortable silence. About forty minutes later, we turn toward a small country road and then continue, passing through a field that's barely drivable. The tall grass obscures most of the view until we arrive in a clearing. The place looks completely isolated. I glance at the tall trees in front of us when Aidan puts the track in the park and turns off the engine. Behind the little forest, I spot sunlight reflecting on an uneven surface and realize there's a lake here. I get a glimpse of a small pier on the side, too, and gasp.

"Wow. How do you know this place?"

"I used to live two towns over for a while as a kid. With one of my aunts. Once, I was wandering around and got a little lost. That's how I found it. Honestly, I've been a little worried if it's still here. I'm glad to see it survived the time because I really want you to see the surprise."

"I thought this place was the surprise?" I point through the windshield and unclasp the seatbelt to exit the car.

Aidan joins me by the door and kisses me softly on the lips. "This is only the first part of the surprise."

"There's more?" I almost yell, and Aidan chuckles at my enthusiasm before moving to grab something out of the back seat. He extracts a blanket and a backpack and then leads me toward the pier.

"Aidan, if I'd known you were planning this romantic date, I would have worn a different outfit," I whine, glancing down at my purple t-shirt with a unicorn, black skirt, and worn-out tennis shoes. I didn't even wear any makeup today.

"Claire, you look beautiful. And it was supposed to be a surprise, so I couldn't exactly tell you, right?"

Aidan goes first to check if the pier is stable enough to sit on and then spreads out the blanket, waving me in to join him. He unzips his backpack and extracts two Tupperware containers and two cans of soda before giving me one.

Something about the fact that he knew not to bring any alcohol warms my heart. I still didn't tell him about the fact that I'm bipolar or that I'm on any kind of medication, which I started to resume taking the day after we met, but he's always so attuned to me. I noticed he stopped drinking whenever we were together. Which is most times, but I know he drinks beer with his gang.

"Hope you're hungry because I brought some food."

"Did you make it yourself?" I eye the pasta inside the plastic container.

Aidan winces, and his face turns slightly pink. "Nah, I wouldn't do that to you. I got it from Hellie's."

"Oh, thank God because I'm starving," I say and grab the extended fork from his palm before digging into it in appreciation. "Don't get me wrong, but after your last attempts at cooking me breakfast..."

He grins and then shovels a big amount of noodles into his mouth with a shrug. "What better way to make your girlfriend swoon than giving her food poisoning, right?"

"Yeah, I was swooning, alright. All the way up to the toilet," I giggle at the memory of puking all over Aidan's bathroom.

Let's just say his brother was not amused when that happened. But at least the whole group of men ran out of the house like the place was on fire, so we had the place all to ourselves for the day. Hence, this is actually a good memory. Still, I'm glad Aidan decided to play it safe when it came to food options for today.

"So, was this the surprise?" I lift my hand with pasta swinging from the fork.

"Nope, the best is yet to come," he says proudly.

"Are we going to go skinny-dipping in the lake?" I guess.

His eyes light up, but he shakes his head. "We can. But that's not the surprise."

I tap a finger on my chin, looking around before I throw my hands up and resume eating. "I give up. I have no idea what the surprise is!"

"Patience, baby."

I'M SITTING COMFORTABLY with my back leaning on Aidan's chest and looking at the calm surface of the water reflecting the last beams of the setting sun when something flickers close to the opposite shore. We've been here for over two hours, talking comfortably, eating and sometimes just relaxing on the blanket after a small make-out session.

"Look," I point to the blinking light and then realize more of them appear closer to us with each second.

Aidan leans his head on my shoulder and kisses my neck. "Here's your surprise."

"Fireflies?" I say in awe and watch as a swarm of insects flies above the lake, illuminating the space in a weird choreography of appearing and disappearing light.

The view is absolutely mesmerizing, and I don't know how long I've been staring at them before I turn to Aidan.

He graces me with one of his shy smiles that I am so familiar with now, and I can't help but kiss him again.

"Thank you. This is the best." I say against his mouth.

"I hoped you'll think so. I wish I could shower you with gifts, and I don't know... jewelry or whatever it is that women like, but I don't really-"

"Shh," I put a silencing finger on his lips. "It's perfect, Aidan. I don't want jewelry or things that money can buy. I just want these moments with you. Nothing else. This is truly the best surprise ever. Okay?"

"Yeah, okay," Aidan relaxes and then grabs his backpack to extract something from the side pocket. "I wanted to show you something. Something that I've made."

I hear the rustle of paper, and my heart speeds up even before he slips it into my waiting hand. Aidan grabs his phone to shine a light on the drawing, and my mouth opens in shock, unable to articulate my words.

It's an image of me sitting on a pier and observing the fireflies above the water. My features are perfectly resembled, and the drawing seems so alive that I have to rub the paper between my fingertips to make sure it's not a photograph.

But it wouldn't actually make any sense. This just happened. I've never been here before.

"How did you know that this is what I will look like?" I lift my gaze from the masterpiece created by my boyfriend.

"I hoped you'd like it and just imagined your face. I know your features, and... Anyway, I have another version on hand in case I was wrong. With your eyes rolling because of how much you dislike my idea of a date."

"Do you really?"

"Nah. I'm joking," he chuckles and grabs the drawing to place it on the side before dragging me back into his arms to lie down with our faces directed at the starry sky with an occasional firefly coming into our view. I snuggle to his chest, slightly choked up with emotions swirling inside me. Is it possible to burst from happiness?

"It's in color," I mutter.

"Hmm?" Aidan hums in question and moves my hair back to glance down at me.

"The drawing. It was in color. The ones I saw before, and the glimpses I got whenever you're working on something... They were all in black. Or dark gray. I didn't see you ever work with color."

"That's because there's no darkness in my mind whenever I think about you, Claire. You're my color. You actually make me excited about my days. I didn't even know just how bleak my life was before you literally slammed into me with your light and your goodness."

"Stop it," I whisper, my lip wobbling. "I'm just a person."

"Maybe for others. But for me, you're so much more," Aidan says confidently before moving to the side and putting his face lower so he can gaze straight into my eyes. "I know it's far too soon to say it, but I think I'm in love with you."

My breath hitches before I can finally share my own feelings. "I'm in love with you too."

CHAPTER VI

WE START OFF BY KISSING slowly. Aidan's lips touch mine so tenderly. Like I'm made of glass, and he's worried that I'll break if he presses any harder. But I need more.

I lower my body to his and flip us both so I'm fully sprawled on him. The strained sound that comes out of his throat when our hips touch motivates me to try something new. I lean back and move my legs on each side of his thighs to straddle him, and quickly get out of my shirt. The chilly evening wind cools my heated skin and makes me shiver.

Aidan's hands move up to get a hold of my hips as he looks up at me with so much desire and love that it melts my heart.

"You're so beautiful, it's fucking insane," he rasps, and I smile genuinely, knowing that he truly thinks so.

I move down a bit to help him get out of his shirt next and press down on his chest when he's trying to sit up and kiss me. His brows furrow in confusion, but all I do is shake my head at him and smile tentatively. I told him how I felt, but now it's time I show him.

I bend down to kiss his neck and then move lower, stopping right above his navel. My hands shake with nerves and excitement when I grab onto his belt.

"Claire, I don't know what you're... You don't have to..." Aidan's voice reaches my ear, and I want to laugh at his failed attempt to try to play a gentleman again. He wants this just as much as I do. I can hear it in the sharp intake of breath he takes.

The knowledge that I have such an effect on him empowers me and helps me shake off the nerves.

I unbuckle his pants, move his black briefs down so he's fully exposed, and then look up at him. His eyes are wide, fully visible in the semi-dark we're coated in, as he watches everything I do. I lick my lips and am pleased with the little groan he makes before I dive in and take the head of his cock into my mouth to suck on it lightly.

If I was worried about him not enjoying it, I needn't have to because the second I bob my head lower to take more of him into my mouth, he hisses, "Holly fuck!". His hands go to my hair, but otherwise, he doesn't stir as I start to move faster and faster.

I can feel his body turn rigid before he moves away, gently pulling me to the side.

"Why did you stop?" I mutter, but in the next second, yelp when I'm flipped to my back.

Aidan kisses me almost harshly; his breathing labored as he reaches under my skirt. My panties are so wet that I know I should be embarrassed about just how much I enjoyed what I just did, but I don't have time for that. His hand moves the obstacle to the side to press one finger into me slowly, and I moan. More, I need more.

I must've said it out loud because Aidan whispers, "You don't have to tell me twice. Take off your bra."

As soon as my breasts are free to the cool air around us, Aidan lowers his head to lick each nipple as a second finger joins to tease me at my entrance. The breeze picks up at that moment to fall on my exposed body, and I tremble from the strange mixture of sensations.

My hand reaches for Aidan, and it's my time to order him to take his clothes off. I'm still in my skirt and have my panties on, but I'm already too impatient to wait any longer. I want him in me. To feel my inner walls closing in on him. To make him possess me as I possess him. I want him to claim me again and again.

When he's too slow for my taste to do just that, I grab onto his face and then sit on his lap. I push my hand between us and move my underwear to the side fully before impaling myself on his hard length.

This is another first for us. I've never been on top before, but I know that I'm going to be back here often from now on. I move my hips, making us both groan in pleasure and then pick up speed, with Aidan's arms helping me move. The perfect pressure his hard cock creates within me at this angle, the amazing sensation on my clit as I'm rubbing against him, and the feel of his hard hot body underneath me built my orgasm up to an incredible level, and when it finally comes, I lose all power in my limbs. Aidan has to catch me to keep me upright as he lifts his hips rapidly, adding to my ongoing inner explosion before he bites lightly on my shoulder as his release comes.

"Holy fuck," he pants and collapses back on the blanket, the wood trembling slightly under.

"Yeah, I agree," I muse and wipe the sweat from my forehead.

Then our eyes meet in the darkness, and we both grin at each other like the fools in love that we are.

"I love you, Claire Thompson."

"And I love you, Aidan Linden."

He lifts his right hand with his pinky outstretched. "Pinky swear?"

I encircle it with my own and laugh, "Pinky swear."

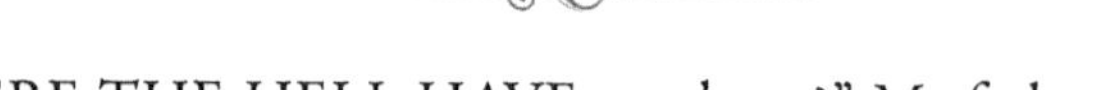

"WHERE THE HELL HAVE you been?" My father booms as soon as I enter the house, and I jump at the sudden volume.

I was sad when Aidan had to drive me back to my house, but since I didn't have a change of clothes and was in desperate need of a shower after everything we'd been doing on the pier, we decided it was best if I come home today. I don't like sleeping without Aidan by my side anymore, but I know I'll see him in a few hours at school.

"Jesus Christ, Dad. What are you doing, creeping around the house in the dark? You scared me. And I was out, obviously," I mutter as I take off my jacket and move past my father, who looks something between enraged and relieved.

"I want you to stop seeing him, Claire. I know you think I'm stupid, but I know you're sneaking off almost every day, and I don't like it."

"It's a shame then that I don't exactly care about your opinions when it comes to my life," I mutter and then frown when he grabs my shoulder to stop me from walking into my room.

"Hey! We have our issues, and I understand your reservations. I do. But I'm still your father, Claire. I worry about you, and your recent behavior shows me that it's not exactly unfounded. Your grades will barely allow you to pass. Your teachers say you don't pay attention. And today, you didn't come home after school and didn't even have the decency to tell me that you're fine. I've been calling your phone for hours. And don't even let me start with that boy..."

I shake my head violently, unable to listen to him trying to play a parent anymore. "I don't want to talk about it. You wouldn't understand..."

I turn and march toward my room, trying to lock myself in, but my father is not having that. He stops me from locking and barges in.

"You will hear this, Claire. That boy you're seeing? Aidan, right? He's dangerous. I asked around. You know what kind of people he associates himself with? Thugs, criminals, drug dealers. He doesn't have a job. He never even came here to introduce himself," I roll my eyes at that and open my mouth to answer, but my father doesn't let me. "This thing between you two seems unhealthy. Your friend runs away, leaving you here with a broken heart, and instead of trying to learn from that experience, off you go find another person to obsess over and jeopardize your future for. Ms. Edwards warned me about something like this happening. You attach yourself to people, making them your whole universe, and when they disappear, you crumble."

"Stop talking about shit that you have no fucking clue about!" I explode and then take a step back, surprised by the force of my rage. My chest heaves with heavy breaths, and my hands shake, eager to claw at him.

My father raises his eyebrows but doesn't react for a while. Then he says in an even voice. "You don't see it that way, but I do want what's best for you, Claire. I was a teenager once, and I know how powerful the first love can be. How destructive. I lived through that with your mother. And I just don't want you to break when it's all over."

"Don't worry. I'm fucking unbreakable," I spit harshly.

My father's shoulders lower with a sigh of resignation as he nods. "God, I hope so. Still, I want you to stop seeing him."

"Get out," I say in a low voice, my lower lip already wobbling with the oncoming tears.

He gives me one last sad look and exits, closing the door behind him.

I swap at the tears angrily and then grab my backpack. After I spill all of my books and school supplies out of it, I open a drawer and grab a few items of clothing. Then I take the only picture of me and my mom I possess, and the frame next to it that presents both mine and Jenny's smiling faces, and open the window. At that point, I don't even care about keeping quiet as I jump over the sill and get out through the back gate.

I've had enough. I don't need my father. All I care about is Aidan. The rest of the world can fucking burn for all I care.

My father's voice calling after me to come back barely registers as I walk through our front yard and disappear from his view around the corner.

He and I are done. He won't keep me away from my happiness. I won't let him.

CHAPTER VII

AIDAN

I wake up and sigh happily like the pussy whipped sap I turned into lately when I feel the small body curled up next to me. Claire's even breaths puff on my naked chest, and I wish, as always, that we can stay like this forever.

It's been three weeks since Claire showed up at my window after the single best night of my life until that point, claiming that she's done with her father. There was no other option for me than to allow her to stay at my place. Saint could grumble about it all he wanted. At this point, Claire became everything that matters in my life.

Although, I admit it's not all a bed of roses living together.

Most days when we can spend the whole day together, Claire is the happy-go-lucky girl I fell for since the moment I first saw her – I'm not ashamed to admit it now after all this time together. We can talk for hours about silly stuff, watch movies or listen to music before making love. Which I won't pretend is not the best part of being together because I could worship Claire's body for hours.

She also loves to watch me draw, which I was reluctant at first to allow her to do. My art is something that is the most intimate part of me. But she built a safe space for me in which I can be myself. So, this became a constant part of our routine as a couple.

I also told her a bit about how it was growing up with an irresponsible mother who cared more about her boyfriends than her own son. She's actually the first person that, I felt, wouldn't judge me for where I come from. Lots of the stories from her own childhood indicate that she also went through some shit with her mom, but it's just something that she throws in here and there.

Life with Claire is good.

However, some days, usually when I have to go run an errand for my brother, I come back to find my girl moody and ready to pick a fight. I know she doesn't like that I'm adamant about keeping her out of that part of my life. But the thought of her looking at me differently or dumping me when she learns the truth, the whole truth, is not something that I can swallow. So, like a fucking coward, I am keeping my mouth shut about the things I know. I'm aware it's going to grow bigger and will eventually cause strain in our otherwise perfect relationship.

And let's not forget about her father, who hasn't been making things any easier for us either. The first week Claire came to live with me and Saint, he's been banging on the door every day demanding to speak with his daughter. To which she refused, of course. And even though he threatened to call the cops a few times, which almost made me panic, he has yet to actually make the call. After all, Claire will be eighteen in two months, and I think her father realizes that if he wants to have any kind of relationship with her, he needs to tread carefully.

Because here's what I learned about Claire. She may seem like this delicate, non-threatening and sometimes clueless person to some, but she's actually anything but. Yes, she is sweet and caring and loves to live in her headspace a lot. But she can be very strong-minded and fierce when something ticks her the wrong way.

Now, I move her tangled golden hair away to kiss her forehead before I slip out of the bed. She still has an hour before she needs to get up for school. Maybe I can surprise her with breakfast or something. This time without poisoning her, hopefully.

I pull on a pair of gray sweatpants, not bothering with a t-shirt, before I exit my room, closing the door behind me soundlessly.

When I get into the kitchen, I'm surprised to see Saint already up. He's holding a steaming mug and staring at the window with a displeased expression on his face.

He's so immersed in his thoughts that I don't think he even noticed me come in, which is confirmed when I open my mouth at last, and he jumps in his seat as if ready to defend himself.

"You alright, bro?" I ask and eye him with real worry.

There's something off about him. He looks like shit and not the hangover, usual type.

"No need to be so jumpy. It's just me," I say, and go to get some eggs from the fridge. My eyes still on Saint.

When he doesn't answer, just gulps heavily and scratches at his unshaven head, I stop my movements.

"Yo, Saint. You okay?" I prompt him again, and this time, his eyes meet mine fully, making me apprehensive.

"I lied to you, Aidy. I lied to the whole gang, actually," he admits.

"About?" I sit opposite him, the thought about the breakfast forgotten. I don't remember my brother ever acting so somber.

"Shit, man. I didn't know..." his lips close, and his jaw flexes. "You were right. I didn't want you to be, but you were fucking right. And I should've listened to your ass. But I thought you were young and scared to do what needed to be done. Turned out that I was the one acting like a clueless bitch."

When all I do is lift my eyebrows, he sighs and looks behind to check if we don't have ears on us. Then he lowers his voice and leans toward me. "Things have been quiet. But you were right to say that they are too quiet after everything. Yesterday, after I dropped the merchandise, I swear I saw someone tailing me. I can't be sure, but he had an undercover cop written all over him. You know the look."

My eyes narrow on my brother, and I nod my head that I understand what he means when he looks around the space. The house could be tapped for all we know.

"Have you called him?" I say, barely under my breath, and Saint grimaces, suddenly unable to look me in the eye.

"What? Santiago, tell me what it is. If you can't, then write it, whatever."

"I lied to you. The boss... He went MIA after... you know. The last job you saw him at."

"What? What the fuck are you talking about? That was almost three months ago, Saint! You told me everything was fine! Who's been giving you orders, then?"

"I kind of have been getting rid of the um... Hoping to do everything we were supposed to as planned, so when he comes back..." He eyes the place again, looking for words that wouldn't incriminate us even worse, and I want to laugh. If the cops are tailing him and that fucker we worked for is gone, then we're already fucking done.

"What are you going to do?" I ask him, my mind already running a mile a minute.

Could I just grab Claire and run with her somewhere where this shit won't touch her? Doubtful. She needs to finish school, and I don't know if she would actually want to leave Bell Ridge. And where would we go anyway?

"Fuck if I know, Aidy. I haven't even told the other guys yet. Maybe it's a false alarm, you know? Maybe we're meant to wait a bit longer. For now, I'll tell the guys to lie low and stop the deliveries. You go to school and act like a normal teenager until we know what is going on. If the cops see us scurrying around like bugs from under a lifted rock, they're gonna be on us. I need at least a week to think of a plan of how to get us out of this fucking town."

"Fuck. Fuck, man. I told you this was gonna happen. And now..." My eyes go to the closed door of my bedroom, and Saint shakes his head.

"You got it bad, brother. I don't blame you. The girl is cute. But next week, we'll be outta here. So you better cut her loose before that."

Cut her loose? My eyes snap to Saint's, but I don't see his usual mean smirk in place.

"Couldn't she come with us?"

"Does she know what we do? Is she aware of the shit we're in?" He questions, not unkindly, but it still sounds like accusations to me.

"She doesn't," I grit through my teeth, and he nods.

"If you can convince her to travel with a bunch of lowlife fuckers, to god knows where, then fine, she can come. I don't care as long as she doesn't become problematic. You would be responsible for her and need to provide or whatever. I don't know if you want to subject her to our way of living, but that's your choice."

My choice. Fuck, I have no idea what to do. But I know one thing. I can't lose her. And it appears that whatever I decide, it can be the end of us.

TURNED OUT, THINKING that we had a week to think about our options was not optimistic but downright naïve.

I've been pulling away a bit from Claire ever since Saint confessed to me, trying to distance myself enough to think about everything and see our relationship from a different perspective. And I know it left her confused with how cold I've been.

But in truth, it only made me realize that I'll have to fess up to my crimes. And do it soon. I can't just leave without telling her the truth. Also, there's a part of me that truly hopes that she'll find it in her big heart to understand my reasons and will forgive me. Maybe even join us and leave Bell Ridge.

After three days of putting it off, I finally decided that today is going to be the day. After picking up Claire from school, I will take her to the pier again and confess.

She's been in a shitty mood, too, lately, and I watch her struggling with putting her clothes on, her movements jerky and impatient, as she's getting ready for school.

"Are you sure you don't want me to give you a ride to school?" I ask from my position on the bed.

Despite Saint's order, I've stopped going to school altogether now, knowing that I won't be finishing high school anyway— at least not in this town.

"No, I told you it's fine," Claire huffs when the zipper on her sweatshirt jams, and she tugs on it.

I get up to grab her hands, and she looks up at me. "Are you okay?"

"Yeah, I'm fine," she presents that fake smile of hers, and I have to refrain from rolling my eyes.

"Clearly not. I'm sorry I was blowing you off the past two days. I just had a lot on my mind lately," I say in a gentle voice, keeping a strong hold on her palms when she tries to retreat from my touch.

"Well, maybe I did too. But you wouldn't know that, right? I mean, you weren't here. You dropped out of school, so clearly, you weren't busy with studies either. I was sitting here at your house. Alone, Aidan. And you didn't pick up your phone. I don't even know what time you came back."

The tears gathering in the corners of her eyes make me feel even worse than I already did. When they spill on her cheeks, I pull her into my arms.

"Hey, baby, don't cry. I told you there was something important I had to think about. I'm sorry that I left. There are just things that you don't know..."

She steps away from my embrace and crosses her arms, looking like a sad puppy. "Why is that, Aidan? Why are there things that you don't want to share with me?"

"No, you've got it wrong. I do want to share everything with you. I do," I press when she shoots me a doubtful look. "I'm scared, okay? I care about you. I love you and want to be with you. You know that. But there's some shit that I've done that-"

My words are stopped by loud bangs coming from the front door, followed by a deafening bang.

Claire jumps back from my bedroom door in fear, and on instinct, I move her behind me, away from it.

Good thing that I did because in the next moment, it bangs open with force as two men in police uniforms step in with their guns raised.

"Madison PD, get on the ground now!" One of them orders, and I drop to my knees.

"Oh my God, what is happening?" I hear Claire cry as she retreats toward the wall that's furthest away.

"Baby, just get on the ground, okay? You're not the one they are looking for. So, they're gonna let you out, but you need to listen to them," I plead with her, barely noticing when the handcuffs land on my wrists after they are yanked behind my back.

Claire kneels slowly with her hands up, her eyes not leaving mine.

"What is happening?" She repeats in a trembling voice.

"I'm sorry. So sorry. I wanted to tell you tonight. I'm so sorry," I start melting as tears come into my eyes. I don't care if I show weakness in front of the officers.

An older man comes into the room, this one wearing a suit. A thick manila folder under his armpit before he looks into it.

"Which one are you then?" He asks without looking at me and flicks through the pages. "Ah! You must be the younger brother, then."

He slams the folder shut and sniffles, eyeing me with cold eyes.

"Aidan Linden, you are under arrest for drug trafficking and drug distribution, as well as cooperation with a wanted fugitive, David Wallace, regarding the attempted murder of a federal agent, arson, and gang activity. You have the right to remain silent. Anything you say can be used against you in court. You have the right to talk to a lawyer..."

Everything else the man is saying gets droned out by the loud ringing in my ears as I watch Claire's body slump down the wall. Her face pales as a silent no leaves her trembling mouth.

The beautiful eyes, usually so full of love and life, dim as she sees the look on my face that shows nothing but guilt and regret. My heart breaks when she chokes on a sob, and I moved my body instinctively, wanting to go to and comfort her.

I'm forced to stand up as one of the cops roughly searches my body for weapons or any other illegal stuff. The older man walks to Claire and offers her a hand to help her stand up with a gentle smile, so at odds with the look he gave me just a second ago.

The commotion from the entryway catches my attention briefly, and I see Saint struggling to get away from the man who's holding him as he kicks and screams obscenities. For a moment, our eyes meet, and he stops fighting. But then he blinks rapidly and resumes his pathetic attempts at getting away with renewed vigor.

I turn my head away, only able to concentrate on what matters the most. All I care to see is Claire. The whole room becomes unfocused as I beg her with my eyes to understand while the cop walks her toward the door.

Please do not give up on me.

But then I see the moment I lose her completely.

Her back turns ramrod straight, her jaw clenches, and her usually warm eyes turn so cold it makes me flinch. I never thought Claire's eyes could express such hatred. Honestly, I thought she was incapable of that emotion.

And the fucked up thing is that she looks so beautiful at that moment. Like a storm cloud right before it strikes out with a bolt of lightning.

"Claire, I love you so much." I throw desperately, my voice sounding alien to my own ears. Everything moves in slow motion.

She only stares at my face before moving past me.

Time moves forward as I watch her say something to the man in the suit, and he nods his head, looking at her with pity. He scribbles something on a notepad and gives her the piece of paper before giving her a fatherly squeeze on the shoulder when she turns to leave.

I feel sick to my stomach. I want to cry, I want to rage, but most importantly, I want to rewind time.

My life as I know it is over. I know prison time is pretty much inevitable.

Yet, all I can think about as I'm dragged through the doorway and pushed out of my house into a police cruiser with my brother and the gang members who were unlucky enough to stay the night is Claire and the cold loathing I saw in her eyes.

I killed our love, and now I'll have to live with that.

CHAPTER VIII

AIDAN - THREE MONTHS ago

I wake up to the loud cheers coming down from the living room and glance at the watch on my wrist. Twelve thirty. Jeez, I've been out of it.

Rubbing at my eyes, I get up and leave my cluttered bedroom barefoot to see what's all this ruckus. Unsurprisingly, I find the guys playing a video game where they have to shoot each other, the whole place fogged up with weed. Saint is nowhere to be seen, but I assume he's the one who let them in. If they even left here since yesterday. Last night is a blur.

"Hey, I'm in here," Saint grumps when I enter the bathroom. He's busy shaving his already bald head until it's literally glowing as always. The guy's obsessed.

"I need to take a piss," I mutter, still groggy from whatever the gang had given me yesterday, saying that it's some kind of rite of passage. I didn't like it.

Saint hums without looking away from the mirror, and after I flush, asks innocently, "Shouldn't you be at school 'lil bro?"

"I don't know, should I?" I ask, not in the mood for his shitty plays. I shove him with my shoulder to get to the sink and wash my hands before I glance briefly at my reflection. I look like shit.

Our eyes meet in the mirror, and Saint smirks before going serious. "Adelaide called."

Mom? I didn't even know Saint and her were in contact with each other.

I try not to show my surprise or any emotion, actually, and shrug. "What does she want?"

One eyebrow slowly lifts on my brother's face at my act of nonchalance before he steps away from the mirror and looks at me directly as he dries his hands on a towel.

"Wanted to know how's things going with her favorite boy, of course. Not me, obviously. Asked if you were doing okay at school and stuff."

I snort, even though the words do bring a painful tightening in my chest. I haven't talked to my mother in years, and now she's calling Santiago. Who's the son she didn't want even more than me, pretending to be the caring mother that she never was?

It's no wonder that the first question out of my mouth is, "What's her deal? Does she need money or something?"

Saint's face brightens, and he laughs before slapping me on my back. "We're so alike, Aidy, it's impossible. That was precisely what I asked her. Took her about ten seconds to hang up."

"Then why are you telling me this?" I eye him suspiciously.

Saint goes back to his solemn look, the tattoo on his neck shifting as his jaw ticks. "Just wanna be always straight with you, *chico*. And remind you that at the end of the day, all you have is me. And the *Culebras*. We got your back. As long as you're with us."

"Okay... thanks," I say lightly, even though his words sound more like a threat than brotherly words of support, and apprehension fogs over my mind for a second.

With a last look thrown his way, I move to get past him. "I'll be in my room. I feel like I need twenty more hours of sleep after that shit you gave me yesterday."

"No can do, bro," his words stop me when I'm in the corridor. "The boss called. He needs us for something. Gotta be at the warehouse in an hour."

"We have a boss now?" I call over my shoulder. "What about *Culebras* being the masters of their own fate and all that shit you told me about before I joined the gang?"

"We were getting nowhere. Wallace will open doors for us. The man has a plan." Clearly, "the boss" is rubbing off on my brother if his delusional words are any indication, and I want to shake some sense into him.

"The man's a fucking lunatic," I say with a sigh, already knowing that Saint won't listen to me.

He's so excited about the prospect of running a drug and gun empire that he's blind to see that the man plotting the whole thing is detached from reality. Yeah, he can use words that will make you believe the giant pile of shit is actually gold, but he won't fool me. I can still smell it from afar.

My mom dated too many twisted men when I was younger for me not to see the signs of barely restrained craziness right away.

"Be ready in fifteen," is all my brother has to say, his voice calm but also again with a little sprinkle of threat underneath.

"Fine." I walk to my room with a shake of my head. Nothing good will come out of the thing we have with Sheriff Wallace. I just know it in my bones.

"DUDE, WHAT THE FUCK is he doing?" I whisper to a guy named Riz as we stand in the half-dark open space of the abandoned warehouse.

There are two empty crates that used to hold some semi-automatics that were already distributed, but other than that, there's nothing here that would indicate what we are here for.

I see the other guys glancing at each other and then toward Saint, who looks unbothered by the weird behavior of the Sheriff, who's busy muttering to himself and constantly checking his phone.

I almost jump when he suddenly stops and laughs at something he sees on the screen before surprising me when he points his finger directly at me.

"You, tall one. We're gonna have company soon. Take care of the guy and bring him here," his eyes look clear at the moment, and his tone is back to normal, but I have no idea what he's talking about.

"I don't..." I start, but Saint cuts me off.

"Hey, man. I don't think Aidan is the best option..." but Wallace is already waving him off.

"It can't be me, and our guest is a big motherfucker. No offense, but all of you wouldn't even reach him to knock him down."

"But-..." Saint tries again, glancing at me nervously, probably scared that I'm going to blow it.

It pisses me off, so before I can think better, I step forward and state, "I'll do it. Tell me what to do."

Pleased, the Sheriff smiles and gives Saint a look before instructing me. The rest of the guys listen intently, too, before Saint's closest friend, Frisco, frowns.

"I don't get it. Is it a guy from the other rival gang you told us about, or what?"

"It's a rival, alright. That's all you need to know for now. It's important for our business to go smoothly to get him out of the equation. Do what I tell you, and you'll see how great things will be getting soon in Bell Ridge." Wallace waves for me to get to it, and I climb on the wooden construction prepared to lift the heavy crates to later put them on top of the giant containers we usually store them in.

The thing was actually my idea, not that anyone thanked me for it. So I know exactly how to get to the window that opens to the rooftop of a small shed. It's high enough to hide me well and covered from two sides but also low enough for me to jump down to surprise whoever will be coming here. There's a lonely plank laying by the leftover pieces of sheet metal, and I grab it in case I need a weapon.

And then I wait. And wait some more.

When I'm actually starting to think the guys pranked me, I see movement coming from the bushes just by the broken fence. And sure enough, a guy big as a fucking house moves quickly toward the warehouse. He looks uncertain, but his moves are smooth and calculated. A zip of adrenalin goes through me as I wait for him to get closer. I watch him checking out the windows, and when he turns away, I realize that this is my moment.

I slip down soundlessly, knowing exactly where to step and how to land, and swing the plank at his head. The guy falls down, and blood starts oozing out of his head. I don't care; too surprised that I actually managed to get rid of the threat.

Letting go of the now bloodied piece of wood, I crouch to check on his pulse and glance up when I hear steps coming closer.

Saint and Frisco see the man laying unconsciously at my feet, and both simultaneously lift their eyebrows before grinning at each other.

"See, man, told you, you've got nothing to worry about. Our little Aidy is growing to be a man," Frisco jabs my brother with an elbow before glancing at me with pride.

Saint looks less impressed but still smiles at me with a shrug. "Let's get him inside then."

It takes three of us to lift him, and I feel my back protesting under the weight. Jesus Christ, who let the Incredible Hulk out in the public?

When we grab him, I notice something falling out of the inside pocket of his jacket and stop my movements.

"Wait! Let's not get sloppy," I groan and let go of his legs to lift what happens to be a wallet. I check out the content briefly and then regret I did. I almost drop the goddamn thing.

"Fuck. He's fucking FBI, dude," I almost yell at Saint.

"What?" He shakes his head and lets go of the unconscious man, too, making him fall to the ground without a flinch. "The fuck he is."

"Check it out," I pass him the wallet and watch his reaction, on the verge of panic. "What if there's more of them, Santiago? We're so screwed. I told you not to listen to this maniac. Gang rivals. Gang rivals, my ass."

Saint blinks twice, his jaw working before his head snaps up from the wallet, and he pockets it. "Doesn't change anything. We have work to do, so we're doing it. FBI or not, he's clearly a guy threatening everything we built so far with the Sheriff." I grab at my hair and eye the body at my feet. "Hey, Aidan! You hear me? Get your shit together and help us carry him in."

I glance at Fresco, who doesn't look pleased but, without a question, grabs onto one of the agent's arms to lift him again. Reluctantly, I grab his legs and wait for Saint to join us.

The chair and ropes are already prepared in the center of the warehouse, and a shiver runs through me. Fuck, if he's set on torturing the man now, I'm out of here. No matter what Saint says about it.

This is already getting out of hand. It's different from being the gang's courier or staying on watch as they are beating some disobedient lowlife dealer for not paying up. But I just assaulted an FBI agent. In fucking broad daylight. This is not what I signed up for.

Cold sweat collects at the collar of my shirt, and I look away from the scene in front of me when the rest of the guys help out situate our victim on the chair.

It takes some time before he wakes, and I see the sheriff brewing with excitement as he glances at the lump-immobilized man sitting in front of him. The maniacal glint in his eye doesn't go unnoticed by me, although I seem to be the only one. The rest of the guys just wait patiently for further instructions, looking at Wallace with a weird kind of respect as if the fact that he was brave enough to go after a federal agent is so admirable.

This is just another proof that I need to get out of this place and far from Saint as soon as I have enough cash stored to buy myself out because you can't just leave a gang.

A part of me doesn't want to do that, doesn't want to give it up because Saint is my only family, and I know I'll be on my own. Yet, I think everyone is right when they say I'm too soft for this life.

I listen as Wallace mocks the guy and rumbles some sick shit about his daughter, and I'm sick to my stomach. This isn't about the gang. This is some personal vendetta shit. And now I'm part of it.

My feet start to back away on their own accord, and I'm almost at the door when Wallace barks some command that I'm too distracted to get, and everyone starts to clear out after me.

An arm encircles my neck before Saint forcefully tugs me down to meet his eye.

"Proud of you, Aidy. But the work is not done. Don't think I didn't see you there, trying to sneak out. There's more to do. We have to make it look like another gang's work."

"Make what looks like another's gang work?" I ask slowly, scared to get the answer.

A dark look crosses over Saint's features. "Do I have to spell it out for you, brother?"

"Yeah, please, do," I untangle myself from his hold forcefully. "Because this shit is not just some petty dealing stuff, Santiago. It gives fucking live-in-prison vibes rather than the 'we're going to be on top' speeches you fed me with."

"Glad to see your balls dropped ultimately, but think again before going against me," my brother rasps as the other guys pass by us with canisters stinking of fuel.

I point my finger at them and start to back away. "I don't care. This is too much. Dealing guns and drugs is miles away from a straight-up murder."

"Is it, though?" Saint crosses his arms, his stance wide. "Good thing that no gun or drug ever killed a man before ain't that right?" He questions, his voice heavy with sarcasm.

"It's different," I reply quietly, and we stare at each other in silence as if we truly saw each other for the first time.

Then my brother sniffles. "Fine. Go home, Aidan. You did your part."

I don't hesitate and turn on my heel right away. The whole way home, I try to convince myself that I didn't just play a part in getting a man slaughtered.

CHAPTER IX

CLAIRE – PRESENT

I'm not sure how did I end up at my house, but I'm glad when the place appears to be empty. There's no way I could look my father in the eye after he warned me about this exact thing happening not even a month earlier. I know he's going to learn everything from the town rumor chain soon enough, but fortunately, I won't be here to face the shame and the pitiful looks of everyone around me.

Poor, stupid, freaky Claire. She actually thought someone loved her. A handsome boy looking at her like she's God's gift. Laughable.

I stumble into the bathroom and open the medicine cabinet above the sink. My shaking hands browse through the shelves and manage to knock down half of the objects. Making my father's stinky bottle of cologne shatter on the tiled floor. The quick, sharp pain barely registers in my frantic mind when a flying piece of glass embeds itself in my exposed ankle. I'm on a mission. On a mission to run, run, run. Run from here and never come back.

Seeing that there's nothing that can help me ease the pain in there, I switch to browsing through the small drawer under the sink and pause when I catch sight of my dad's razor.

Grabbing the small plastic handle, I eye the three blades aligned in the small frame and then close the still-open cabinet to face the mirror.

My face looks unfamiliar like it's somebody else staring at me through the reflection. An impostor taking over my body and fooling me into believing that I could have a happily ever after. That a person is able to accept me as I am, be truthful, and shower me with love.

I've been an unwanted fruit of a broken relationship between a mentally ill nineteen-year-old girl and a simple-minded trucker who married her on the whim while riding through Vegas one time. Did I really stand a chance in life? A life full of disappointment, abandonment, and death. How could I assume that there's someone out there who will be above that and take me away on the wings of love?

It never ends, does it?

It will only end when you take matters into your own hands.

How long did my brain play tricks on me? Was it after I stopped taking my meds for some time? Making myself vulnerable for the illusions to wiggle their way in.

Was anything that Aidan said true? Or did he see this pathetic creature that I am and decided to toy with the broken girl? Torture her with promises of a life together.

And what about Jenny? Where was she when I was being used and manipulated? Why did she leave me here alone, vulnerable, free for bad people to prey on me?

Maybe she was relieved when she could finally leave me behind. Maybe she was playing, too.

The sad truth is I have no way of knowing for sure what is real to anyone, and it's the most crushing feeling in the world. Why can't I be the master of my own feelings and my own truths?

"I need to know that whatever happens, you'll be all right. I need to know I still have you somewhere in the world. Safe and sound. Can you promise me that? No matter what?"

Well, it turns out some promises are meant to be broken; isn't that the truth, Miss Wallace? You weren't here. You left me to fend for myself. You left me to search for love elsewhere.

Fuck Aidan. And fuck Jenny. And fuck my pathetic excuse of a father. He's a goddamn disappointment, too.

I'm done fighting. I'm done struggling to make sense of everything that's around and of what's my brain trying to conjure up all the time. I know it's time to flee.

Still holding on to the razor, I lower myself into the empty bathtub and slowly, not to cut my fingertips, break apart the little instrument to extract one sharp blade. They're small, but I know if I press hard enough, they will help me escape.

My brain is veiled with a heavy fog of despair, and I honestly don't even register the pain at the first deep cut. As I switch to the other hand, I can already see the crimson stream covering my sleeves in a rapid tempo, and I smile.

There will be peace and lightness as soon as I break away from this treacherous body.

I'm trying to move to my other wrist to do the same, but the razor slips from my bloody fingertips, landing between my thighs. I stare at it and concentrate on my slowing heartbeat. My quiet intakes of breath.

My vision gets blurry with white spots, and I feel lightheaded, so I give in to the cold, numb feeling flooding me, making me feel as if I were submerged in cold, clear water.

A series of images enters my mind, playing as if in slow motion, yet passing so fast it all blurs into one.

My grandfather rocking me on his bony knee in our small wooden house back in Alaska. Him preparing me breakfast consisting of scrambled eggs and freshly baked bread every morning. His gentle smiles whenever I said something childishly funny or learned something new. Then, his last glance at me playing in the garden as he was chopping wood before he fell to his knees, his hand squeezing his chest.

My mom was crying in the corner and walking around as if she were a ghost long before she passed. The little, insincere smiles she gifted me with whenever I was trying so hard to make her laugh. I wanted to be her sunshine and bring her joy, so I pretended to be cheerful even when I was really sad. And she pretended that it took her pain away. I remember her purple toes, bent unnaturally, swinging back and forth, her body hanging from the beam under the ceiling.

"I'm coming, Mom," I whisper, and see her smiling face. She appears in front of me, looking just as she was on her good days. The free way, she danced in the garden in her simple floral dress. Her hands reach toward me, inviting me to join her.

I was never angry with her decision to leave this world because, I guess, on some fundamental level, I always understood what needs to happen to people like us. What do we need to do to end the suffering.

I grab onto her soft palms, the touch filling me with warmth. The relief I feel is immediate, but then I notice someone else behind her. Someone who doesn't have the right to interfere in this happy moment. I see Aidan looking down at me, his face disappointed. His mouth moves rapidly, but I don't understand the words he's saying. His sad eyes draw me in, and I lose sight of my mother. Then I feel the last painful tug on my heart before my eyelids close.

"Oh, my God, Claire!" I hear a bang from a distance, and then...

Silence.

THERE ARE NO WORDS to explain the feeling of disappointment I experienced after waking up to the sound of my beating heart registered on the annoying monitor. There's no way to describe the anger at being stripped of the only way out.

Yet, people act like I should be grateful. Like I should apologize. That's laughable. They should apologize to me, actually. Was it not my choice to be free? Was I asking to be brought back after, at long last, getting peace?

No. I've been ripped from the black stillness—the wonderful void of nothingness.

Six minutes, they said. My heart stopped for six fucking minutes before they brought me back. A miracle, one doctor even dared to say.

So, now, here I lay. Immobilized, with both my arms and legs strapped to the bed, after being brought from the ICU to the psych ward. Staring at the white ceiling with an annoying chipped part in the shape of Africa. It drives me nuts.

The medical staff comes and goes. Probing at me, asking questions that I can't respond to truthfully if I ever want to be free of here, before drugging me with some heavy shit.

I know my father visited me a few times, but I don't acknowledge him. He doesn't have a place in my life. He's been exiled for calling the ambulance after he found me. In my book, it's unforgivable.

I heard him crying each time at my bed and even felt him grabbing at my hand, but I didn't care. The part of me that cared died in that bathtub. And I'll do everything I can to never be that girl again.

Never again.

CHAPTER X

AIDAN - THREE YEARS later

"Linden, you're up!" I hear the harsh voice of one of the guards before he stands in front of my cell, looking at me with cold indifference. "Grab your personal stuff, and step out."

The zing of restless energy fills me up to the brim, and my hands start shaking when I go through my stuff like I haven't already prepared everything for my departure. I look around wildly, to see if I didn't leave anything of value here, which is laughable because apart from my art, I don't have objects worth saving. I don't bother grabbing the essentials and hygiene products, thinking they're shit prison quality anyway, and I would purchase better stuff when I'm out.

Putting the neat stack of drawings separated into two overstaffed folders under my armpit, I turn toward the guard when he makes a sound of impatience.

"Don't have all day, Linden," he rumbles, and I nod quickly before stepping out in front of him.

I'm glad it's this guy who will be walking me out. He may not be the most pleasant person to be around, but at least you can tell he's a good guy in general. Some of the guards here... Well, let's just say that there really is a thin line between being the ones that are in the cell versus those that are just outside those bars.

They thrive on the little power that they are given here and love to humiliate fuckers like me who just want to get by each day. And don't even let me start on the illegal shit they are pulling here on the daily.

So, yeah, the only difference between those who are doing time here and some of those guards is that the imprisoned guys got caught. That's it.

The man standing in front of me now gives me a quick once over and then motions with his head to follow him.

Remembering to keep my head down, I walk close by, praying that no one will start anything just as I'm about to head out.

You constantly hear those stories, and it's what kept me up through the night. The dread of an inmate starting a fight, a crooked guard pulling some shit just because he can, or just a jealous guy causing trouble, so you're unable to get out in time.

If you miss the release date, you have to wait for the protocol to start anew, and I can't imagine the disappointment I would have to face if I didn't make it outside today.

It's been three years, two months, and ten days, and I don't intend on spending any more time than necessary here.

Fortunately, we made it out of the cell block without any disturbances, besides some menacing words and slurs thrown from all sides, but I didn't even hear it. The buzzing in my ears stops any coherent sound from getting to me.

When we enter the prison warden's office, I am told to strip before the whole bend and cough derogatory procedure takes place. The same one I had to go through when I was being admitted all those years ago and a few times after my mom visited me. I want to ask the three guys that circle around me why do I have to do that shit if I'm getting out, but I'm so scared, thinking that even a wrong look from me would mean I'm being sent back in. So, all I do is stare at my toes and wait for this nightmare to be over.

After signing a ton of papers, my personal belongings from the time I was first admitted are provided to me in a zip-lock bag, and I want to laugh for some reason. I wouldn't even recognize these things as mine after all this time.

A black generic-looking wallet, a cell phone with a broken screen, clothes that surely won't fit me anymore, what's with me gaining some muscle, and a heavily creased photograph of me and a girl who years ago grabbed my heart and never let go of it.

A girl who was already lost to me from the first time our roads crossed. I knew it back then but was stupidly hoping that somehow I could still change the inevitable if the stupid lovesick look on my face is anything to go by. I thought I could distort the past with just the power of my want for her.

But it didn't happen. And now, I'm here.

Starting over. Without the girl, without family, friends, work, or pretty much anything that I could have had at the age of twenty-two, if I hadn't been so fucking stupid.

For a small second, I battle with the ridiculous thought of smacking the guard standing in front of me just so they could lock me up again and throw away the key. The fear of facing what's waiting outside is so strong.

But of course, I stopped this weird impulse immediately, the need to get out of this place overpowering everything else.

Another man comes into the room, this one dressed in a nice suit and lifts his chin at his colleagues in a silent question.

"He's good to go," one of the meaner guards chirps and then slaps me on the shoulder with enough force to make me wince but not enough to make me lose balance if that's what the jerk was hoping to happen.

The other guy gives him a nod and then, in an official voice, addresses me directly.

"Aidan Linden, you are getting released, but it is my duty right now to remind you that you are still undergoing your sentence until it expires. While on your parole, you are to contribute to the community as your parole officer deems appropriate. If at any time you break the law requirements for your release, you will return to this correctional penitentiary to continue the rest of your sentence. Today, after getting transported from the facility, you will meet with your parole officer to discuss the details. Do you understand?"

Shit, it's really happening, I'm getting out. I can feel a small drop of sweat collecting at my nape before it slowly travels down between my shoulder blades. My mouth turns dry, and I can barely manage to say yes, my voice sounding alien to my own ears, but the warden nods quickly and claps his hands.

"Right. Officer Simmons, please escort Mr. Linden to the exit," then the older man pins me with a look as if ordering me to behave and leaves the room.

The guy who slapped my back shoves me not so gently toward another door, this one bigger, as if he wants to relish in his last minutes when he can overpower me.

Like a docile child, I hang my head low and go, trying to control my heavy breathing. I ignore every other sound, focusing fully on the tiles of each corridor the asshole is pushing me through as I squeeze my belongings to my chest.

I count each step I'm taking, and when I'm at a hundred and twenty, the fresh air hits my face. I look up at the sunny sky in wonder.

Yeah, we were allowed to walk around the prison yard every day for a limited time, but somehow, it's different from there. Gray, sad, and cold.

Now, I close my eyes, trying to soak in the warm rays, smiling for the first time in... in three fucking years. I almost fall to my knees, wanting to bawl like a baby, but snap out of it when the guard reminds me of his presence.

He jabs his meaty finger toward a giant parking lot. "Wait there with other fuck-ups." And then looks at me with a cruel gleam in his eye. "Till next time, princess."

Despite knowing better, I can't stop myself from snapping at him. "There won't be a next time."

Right away, I start to stiffen, thinking I just blew everything, and he's going to take me back through the door I just came out of.

But surprisingly, the guy just laughs. "Yeah, like I haven't heard that one before."

After serving me one last mocking glare, he turns and slams the door after him.

Right away, I do as I'm told, worried that they are probably watching me, and march in the pointed direction. When I get closer, I'm surprised to notice a small bench next to a bus stop post, with two guys already sharing the narrow space and two other guys standing separately, each of them wearing the same mask of confusion, relief, and fear I'm probably presenting right now too. I step close but leave a safe distance, giving them all a slow nod.

The two sitting at the bench look exactly like someone who would be associated with my brother, the tattoos on their faces similar to the ones Saint was sporting. They both give a small chin lift in response before they continue with their silent conversation.

Within the next thirty minutes, another guy joins us but doesn't acknowledge anyone as he continues to stare at his feet until the time when the bus arrives. We enter the vehicle, and the whole ride is silent, even the two guys who were conversing earlier fully focused on the landscapes passing behind the bus windows.

I'm mesmerized by the simplest things, and my hands itch to draw literally everything, but all I do is squeeze the bag I'm holding along with my drawings, making the plastic creak loudly, and continue to stare.

It's like you remember what the world looks like, but at the same time, you forget. Hard to explain, but it's one of the most bizarre feelings in my life. Observing things that normally wouldn't even make me blink twice, with a new set of eyes, as if I was born anew today.

The bus takes us to Downtown Madison and stops in an almost empty parking lot next to a small building that has already seen its better days. As the doors of the bus open, I notice for the first time that there's indeed a driver with us. I was too preoccupied with my internal freak out about being outside to even notice him. The guy looks like he's a short walk from getting a heart attack as he stumbles heavily out of the cabin.

"'Ight, this is the Probation Division. Out you go, fellas," he wheezes with the heavy voice of a smoker and gets out, only to immediately light up a smoke. He wipes the sweat from his forehead and nods his head toward the building when all we do is stare at him. "Off."

This time, the six of us jump to our feet and exit the stifled interior of the bus. I take a deep breath but regret it on the spot as the fumes and smell of the city hit the back of my throat.

Muttering a curse, I follow the others into the building, where we're quickly assigned a number of a cubicle we are meant to enter to meet with our new probation officer. I knock on the half-wall that displays my number and raise my brows when I see that it's a female sitting behind the small desk that is almost bending under the weight of scattered papers. She's very good-looking and elegant, which is in complete contrast to how this place looks, and I wonder what a person like her is doing working in this shithole.

She looks up from a document she is reading, and I instantly get my answer when her eyes latch onto my torso and arms and then study my face in a weird, predatory way.

What the fuck? I feel fucking naked.

"Aidan?" She asks, and I nod. "Have a seat."

I plop gracelessly into the seat opposite her and look around, trying to avoid her weird stare before I drop my things next to the feeble chair that squeaks under my weight.

"So," she claps her hands when the silence gets almost unbearable, and I start to shift in my seat. "Attempted murder of a police officer, arson, and gang activity. Phew, that's a nice crime sheet."

This time my eyes snap to hers, and I give her an "Are you fucking joking?" look, to which she giggles.

She smacks her red lips and looks down at the document she's holding. "Getting out on parole after three years. Wow, someone must've had a good day within the justice system. Lucky you!"

I clear my throat and decide to speak. "You were meant to tell me what I will have to do to not be thrown back in?" I try to regulate my voice, but the small tremor gives my nerves away.

"Oh, pshh," she waves a hand and laughs. "Right to the chase, huh? Okay. Well, Aidan, the first step would be for you to get a job. Since it seems you already got one, the next thing you do is get a place to live, where I can visit to see if your resocialization process is going smoothly. Once a month, we do a summary of your progress, yada yada, boring red tape bullshit stuff, and you avoid anything that could lead you toward breaking the law again or any type of offense. Oh, and you can't leave the state without my permission, which would only be given if you have a good reason. Got it? Great..."

"Wait, you said I have a job? I don't..." I shake my head just as a knock resonates behind me.

My parole officer jumps excitedly to her feet like it's Christmas and Santa Claus just entered through the chimney. I wonder if she's just overenthusiastic and loves her job or if she's mentally challenged. I heard plenty of stories from other inmates about their parole officers being bonkers.

"Oh, hi..." She gives the visitor a similar appraisal look that I received at first, and I'm somewhat relieved that it just seems to be her M.O., and maybe she's not set on seducing me. Which wouldn't be bad in normal circumstances, but everything is far from normal right now.

"Sandra, you look lovely as always," the deep voice responds, and finally, I look up from my slouched position to glance at the guy and then leap as if I were electrocuted. My breath gets stuck in my lungs as all the blood leaves my face.

Jesus, this day just won't stop throwing emotional curveballs at me. I almost miss the simplicity and predictability of the prison. I've been out for like two hours, and the reality just can't stop smacking me in the face.

The man I last saw in the courtroom, the man I nearly helped get murdered. Damon Brody is standing in front of me with a knowing smirk on his face.

I struggle to stand up, but when I do, I am quickly reminded that if it were a fair, one-on-one fight with this guy, he would snap me in half with the sheer advantage of his giant posture and the size of his muscles.

I worked out plenty in my cell, and I've gotten a lot bigger, but I still look like a twig next to this giant.

We eye each other for a minute, and soon, my look of terror transforms into a frown.

The guy still looks like a fucking Terminator, but you can see that those almost four years took their toll on him. His hair started to turn grayish right at his temples, and a few deep lines were added to his face. I notice the walking stick he grabs onto with a tight fist as if he's worried that without it, he's going to keel over. Involuntarily, I give him a questioning look as if to ask him if I'm responsible for that one, too, but all I get is a grin before he chuckles.

"What is it, man? You look as if you had just seen a ghost."

I open my mouth to respond, but no sound comes out of me as I continue to stare. What do you say in a situation like this? I never thought I would see him again, hoping... I don't know what I was hoping, but he's the last person from my past that I thought I'd bump into.

"That's so fucking hot," Sandra whispers, which helps me snap out of it as I give her an incredulous look. Again, what the fuck is wrong with that woman?

If Brody heard that, he doesn't show it as he steps into the cubical, occupying all that was left of the already small space.

"Have a seat, Damon," Sandra motions to the empty chair next to her, but he just waves her off.

"I'll better stand; you know what's with the leg..." he smiles charmingly and taps the stick on the side of his leg quickly.

She blinks as if she's mesmerized by his presence before sitting down in her own chair.

"Of course, of course," then she seems to remember that she has a job to do other than to ogle men, and again grabs the papers. "So, as I already informed Damon earlier on the phone, I approved the provided workplace as well as the position of a general laborer..."

"Wait, I didn't apply for anything yet..." I muse as I sit back down.

She glances at the big man again and then smiles at me. "Well, you should be glad then that you got the job so easy, Aidan. Most ex-convicts really struggle with finding stable positions after their release. Now, you have one thing less to worry about. I would say that it's awfully generous of Damon to first write the letter to the Parole Commission and then even secure a job for you. That man has a big heart."

"What? What the fuck are you talking about?" I explode and look between those two people, wondering what kind of sick game they are playing.

"Calm down, Aidan. That's not a way to speak to a lady, now, is it?" Brody throws a threatening glare my way that makes me mutter a quick sorry toward Sandra before he continues. "I run a construction company. It's not that big, but I need people. You need a job to start again. If I were you, I wouldn't overthink it. This is probably the only chance that you will get to restore your life that quick."

"But what's the catch?" I ask with a glare of my own.

"There's just one, really. Don't make me regret it because if you cross me, there won't be getting out again. I'll make sure of it. You'll be making a full sentence, and we both know that if that happens, you won't get out before you're forty. So, all I ask is that you come, do your job, and don't get in my way."

"Yeah, okay. But why?" I press, unable to just let it go. I wasn't born yesterday. If this is some kind of revenge plan he came up with, he better think again because I'm not falling for his bullshit.

Brody presses his lips together as if he's on his tail end of being patient. "Why what?"

"Why are you doing this? After everything I've put you through. You must fucking hate my guts. And here you are, offering me a job and a letter to the Parole Commission? What's that about, man?"

I don't know what he sees when he looks at me, but something close to pity crosses his face, and I don't fucking like it.

"Sandy, would you be so kind to leave us for a minute?" He asks my parole officer, who's been watching all of this unfold as if she was just watching her favorite soap opera. All that's missing is some popcorn in her lap.

She jumps to her feet and goes around the desk. "Of course, of course. Take all the time you need, Damon."

He shuffles to the side to let her pass, but she still ends up rubbing against him as she exits. Her hips give an extra sway as she continues down the corridor.

If this was happening anywhere else, I would snort at her overtly sexualized behavior, but since I'm left alone with the only guy who is fully entitled to hold a grudge against me and to want to destroy me, I hold it in and just frown when he falls into the chair that Sandra just vacated.

"What about your leg? I thought you couldn't sit?"

Brody gives me a knowing look and smiles with a shrug.

"Well, Sandra is mostly harmless. And she's good at her job; despite the flirty act, she actually cares. But sometimes, she struggles when it comes to boundaries, so I try to keep my distance. The woman has some serious daddy issues, so if you're thinking about it. Don't."

"I wasn't," I grimace. "Honestly, this is the last thing on my mind right now."

Brody leans forward a bit, resting his forearms on the cane.

"Glad to hear it. So, you want to know why I'm helping you," he says with a sigh and then gives me an analyzing look as if to check how much can he tell me.

He scratches the stumble on his cheek and looks to the side for a moment before he starts to speak. "I was angry, man. So fucking angry when it all went down. If I were to be the one making the decision back then, all of you would face life in prison. I didn't care who you were, why you did what you did, and who came up with which idea. I lost so much because of that day. I lost my job, a big chunk of skin, my self-respect, and most importantly, my girl. I hated you, and I hated myself for letting that bastard fool me." His fists clench on the small handle of the walking stick, and all I can do is gulp, hoping that he won't beat me to death with it within the next five minutes. But then he relaxes his posture and looks back at me with a serious expression. "For a time, after I was released from the hospital and during all those court sessions, I was obsessed with all of you. With finding Wallace. With getting my revenge. When you were all sentenced, it eased just a bit, but I still kept tabs on you and your friends."

"They're not my friends," I spit out, a little too harsh.

One of Brody's eyebrows lifts, but he doesn't comment, set on continuing with his story.

"After a time, along with my pain, some of the hatred eased out even more, and I was able to look at the events of that night with clearer eyes. I remembered the faces, who said what, and that sort of thing. You weren't there in that warehouse, right?" He asks, and it's not really a question, but I still shake my head no.

"But I was the one that knocked you down..." I say, lowering my gaze, not being able to look at the guy any longer. The resentment I hold for that one moment that changed the course of my life irreversibly remains in me, like a venomous snake swirling around in my blood, poisoning me.

"Yeah, I know. I remember your testimony. And I remember your file." He taps the cane on the floor two times to get my attention and then slowly asks. "You were never given a chance, did you, kid?"

I'm not exactly sure what he means by that, and I frown, unable to answer, but I guess he's not waiting for one because he starts speaking again, this time, his tone getting even more wistful.

"You see, I didn't have a stable childhood. And my parents weren't so great at taking care of me, but still, I was given a chance. I was taken in by my aunt and uncle, who were good people. Then I almost died, but still, the universe gave me a chance to try to fix it all. I lost someone very important, and yet I received another shot when I found her. Last year, we both almost died, which would be equal to leaving our son. And we're lucky to still have people in our lives who would take care of him, but it got me thinking. What if we didn't? What if there was no one to give him the same chances that I seem to be receiving again and again? What happens to young people that literally have no one to offer them the help when they need it the most?"

"So, what, I'm some kind of project for you just so you can feel like the scales are more even 'cause you're giving back what you received?" I mock, trying to navigate quickly through the things he told me. That sounds nice and all. But it's too nice. No one does anything without the possibility of gain. "Am I to believe that you are actually helping me from the goodness of your heart?"

"I don't care what you believe in, Aidan," Brody says sharply, done with the storytelling act. "I expect you to be on time, do your job, and not get into trouble. That's the chance I am willing to give you. It's up to you what you decide to do with it."

With that, he stands up with way more agility than you could expect from someone of that posture and with a fucked up leg at that.

"Sandra will give you my company address and my phone number. I expect to see you at eight in the morning sharp. Don't worry about clothes or tools; you'll get that when you show up."

"But I don't know anything about construction..." I mutter toward his retreating back. I can see the inhale he takes before he throws over his shoulder.

"See you tomorrow," and then he limps away, darting between the cubicles.

I frown at my knees, mulling over everything, when Sandra enters, balancing two cups of coffee in both hands. She looks around the small office before her lips downturn.

"Oh, is he gone already?" She asks in disappointment, and I jump to help her with one of the cups. "Oh! Aren't you a gentleman? You can have the coffee then."

"Um, thank you," I sit back down and take a small sip.

Sandra takes back her seat and rests both of her elbows on the desk, her attention fully on my face again now that the target of her worship is absent.

"Now, let's talk about housing..."

CHAPTER XI

My head bobs to the sultry song that fills my eardrums, and I do a little swirl behind the counter before asking yet another sleazy-looking guy in his obvious midlife crisis stage what is his poison of choice for tonight.

I get his order done and deliver it with a flirty smile, even though I cringe inwardly at the way he licks his lips and eyes my cleavage.

It always baffles me that some men coming to the Pink Panther would rather hit on the bartending girl dressed modestly compared to the waitresses and dancers all around them. I mean, just now, my friend Trixy is taking off her bra and shaking the goods in some guy's face before swaying around the pole set in the middle of the stage.

When I started to work as a bartender in a strip club about two years ago, I was certain that I'd be in the clear because of all the beautiful semi-naked women walking around while I was staying hidden in the shadows, preparing drinks. But I was wrong.

Men always want what they can't get. It excites them more when you're not interested. And unfortunately, they love it when you play hard to get. I say, unfortunately, because it's not an act in my case. I'm not interested. Sometimes, I even think that I turned asexual because no one can get me interested since...

Nope. Not going there. I must be getting sober again.

I motion to the other girl working next to me, whose name is Cassy, that I'll be back in five before I slip through the backdoor and flinch at the harsh light and sudden silence as always when I reach the soundproofed part of the club.

I enter the changing room for the stripping girls, where I also store my things, and check to see if I'm alone before diving for the little baggy that contains the powdered happiness that's been keeping me going for years now.

My nose burns slightly after I snort two neat lines from the little mirror I carry around, but the feeling is quickly overpowered by the euphoria flooding my body within my next breath.

There will be time for shame and self-disgust tomorrow when I run out of my stash, but now nothing else exists than the beautiful feeling of happiness.

I go back behind the bar and finish my shift, bouncing around like an over-energized bunny, and sing every lyric to each song that plays on the stage.

I'm free, and no one can take that away from me right now. Not Cassy, who keeps shaking her head at my antics, not Trixy when she comes off the stage and shoots me a worried glance that I'm too distracted to acknowledge, and not all the leery men around me.

This is Claire's time, and right now, I'm on top of the world.

It's after two in the morning when the bouncers straighten their poses, and the waitresses rush to look even more busy as the club's owner comes through the entrance, his younger brother in tow.

Sergio and Nico Ramirez are both big, dangerous-looking men dressed in expensive suits, but as soon as you watch their dynamics, there's no question as to who's the real boss here.

I only had one interaction with Sergio when he ordered for someone to bring him some Scotch to the back office. And I've been avoiding even looking at him directly ever since.

The man is handsome, I'll give him that, but the look in his eyes did nothing to hide his ugly nature. It was something that I encountered before. Cold calculation, cruelty, and evil thoughts. I remember that same look crossing through David Wallace's eyes many times whenever he glanced at his daughter before masking it with a good-natured smile. But the older Ramirez brother never bothers to hide it. He doesn't have to. He's dangerous, and he wants everyone to know that.

His younger brother, Nico, is a tame version of his brother who doesn't hold the same level of ugliness within him, but there's no doubt in my mind he would do everything Sergio asked him for. It's like he's a puppy waiting for his brother's approval.

Together, they own a chain of very well-known bars and strip clubs in Chicago.

I guess, at one point, Nico developed a small crush on me, which became apparent when, instead of getting me fired from the previous location for cursing out a client and dropping a drink in his lap, he just moved me to the Pink Panther, where he frequents more often.

We sometimes flirt, but I do try not to string him along too much. I can't downright shoot him down because I need this job. But I'll never be interested. So, I've been waiting for him to get bored with me and move on to the next girl while playing nice.

Now, his eyes find me right away, and he winks before snapping his head away to nod solemnly at something his brother says. I watch as they disappear behind the double doors, protected by one of the guards.

The whole staff seems to take a collective breath of relief as we all get back to our task, the clients obliviously drooling at a woman named Mila hanging upside down from the pole with her legs spread wide.

By five in the morning, the place is getting empty, and most waitresses look worn out and ready to get home. Saturdays are usually the worst for them. Not me, though. I've been having a great time, with two more trips to the backroom.

Finally, at six, we close after the last customer and start cleaning the place. My smile still in place; I finish tidying the bar in no time and am soon helping around other girls with the tables and polishing the stage.

When I exit the building, it's already eight in the morning, and the sun beats restlessly at my blond hair. The last remnants of my high are starting to wear off, and heavy drops of sweat collect at the top of my forehead before running down my temple.

I frown at the once again ugly-looking world around me and begrudgingly start walking toward the small apartment that I rent with my friend Christy.

As soon as I open the door, the rancid smell of puke welcomes me, and I rush to the sofa where a limp, skinny body lies with her head hanging from the edge—a splash of vomit on the floor, with chunks of it sticking to her tousled hair.

"Shit. Christy? Christy! Wake up," I shake her forcefully, scared shitless that this time she surely overdosed, but then almost collapse in relief when she stirs and groans.

I help her flip to her back and curse loudly when I notice the needle still sticking out of her arm. The purplish veins in her pale skeleton arm alarm me even more. I take a brief look around and find a burnt spoon and a lighter.

"I thought you were done with this shit, Chris. It's fucking killing you," I blink back the tears of despair and set myself on anger instead. "What the fuck were you thinking? You could've choked on your own puke."

She coughs a few times before mumbling something unintelligible and then falls asleep.

I rub my forehead and close my eyes, regretting the last portion of coke blown up my nose prematurely. I could sure use the boost right now.

Feeling the heavy weight of depression looming over me, I turn Christy's head in case she needs to throw up again and then get to my room, which looks as if a hurricane swept through it. I toss the jumble of clean and dirty clothes from my bed and crawl under the comforter.

Even though my body is tired, and I know sleep would be the best remedy, I end up staring at the ceiling for what feels like forever. My eyes are bleary but dry, even though I feel like I could cry forever.

What happened to me? How did I get to this point? And with the way things are going with Christy lately, will I be saying goodbye to another friend again?

Is Christy even my friend?

We met during my stay in the psych ward, and she was in the same therapy group as me—a group for suicidal kids with mental illnesses. Christy has a borderline personality disorder. She was also struggling with anorexia for years before deciding to take her life by swallowing a bunch of pills.

At first, we didn't seem to see eye to eye because she hated my constant smile and the way I used to hide my pain behind the sweet girl exterior. Christy called me a phony many times during our sessions together.

With time, we became friends, but because the doctors didn't want us to become too dependent on each other, they signed us up to different groups. It didn't change much. We still saw each other during our spare time and other group activities, and it was Christy who waited for me outside the hospital when I was discharged.

We decided to give up on school or going back to our families and move to Chicago together, where Christy's cousin Riley had a job waiting for both of us at the strip club. As soon as we rented the place and I sweated out the last remnants of the meds that they pumped me with for over six months, I started to struggle big time. I didn't sleep, I didn't eat, and I barely got out of bed.

That's when Christy decided to introduce me to my new way of living.

"Look, you struggle with highs and lows, yeah? So, listen, there won't be any lows if the highs never end, right?" Christy waved a little plastic bag in front of my face, her eyes already glassy from snorting a line not a minute before.

"I don't think that's a good idea, Chris. What if I get addicted?" I bit my lip with worry. I've never done drugs before. I didn't even like to smoke weed with Jenny because it made me feel even worse.

Christy snorted and rolled her eyes at me. "According to the wacko doctors, you're supposed to take meds until your last breath, Claire. Do you think that's any different? It's all the same stuff, but the pills had the fun part removed from them, so what's the point?"

And that's how it began.

It was working great for a year or so. We've been having fun together. Working at the club, with me as the bartender and Christy as a stripper. We used what we made for rent, bought minimal amounts of food, and used the rest to splurge on more cocaine. After work, we would close ourselves in the apartment and watch movies, play video games, or have a dance-off. I thought life couldn't be any better.

But then the highs began to waver. Last shorter. It was harder to reach that blissful state for hours to come. And the lows were getting even lower.

It was then that Christy started to mix things up, looking for something stronger, more potent, and cheaper. I didn't like it and was very vocal about that.

With time, our friendship fell off the rails completely. Christy only being civil whenever she's high nowadays.

She started to lose weight, and after a while, even some of her teeth fell out. It took one look from Sergio and Nico at her pathetic state to throw her from the club like she was nothing.

It's been downhill from that point on. And there's nothing I can do about it. I'm in it myself, even though I do always find excuses for the way I've been living. I need it to survive, and after all, I'm nowhere near Christy's state.

But am I really better than her? The answer is no.

When I can no longer keep my eyes open, after hours of boiling in my miserable thoughts and oncoming memories, I feel myself getting dragged to sleep.

As always, the last thing that I see are the eyes of a boy who held my heart in the palm of his hand, only to crush it into tiny pieces. He still holds the shards, and I worry he'll never let them go, so they could never be sewed back together.

CHAPTER XII

GOING TO WORK ON TUESDAY was a challenge. I've spent the last two days barely doing anything besides cursing myself for snorting all my money up my nose a week before my paycheck. The tips from customers were scarce on Saturday because I've been too busy having fun with myself and staying in the Lalaland rather than focusing on the men and drawing money from their grabby hands.

I'm so angry at myself. At the situation. At my fucking life, and useless brain, and the people who left me or let me down.

I heard Christy moving around the place at some point on Sunday and leaving before returning with a guy later. I couldn't bring myself to face her or whatever it was that she was doing to get drugs. Yesterday, she went out without even checking up on me, which made me even more depressed, and she hasn't been back ever since.

The shift starts as usual, but my movements are sluggish, and I know most men find my standoffish behavior off-putting because as soon as they get their drinks, they are off to make friends with the dancers. No one lingers, and I'm honestly glad for that.

Halfway through the shift, the older Ramirez appears from the backdoor, waving in a bouncer, looking agitated, and I feel my eyebrows pulling down.

Has he been at the club this whole time? I don't remember there ever being a time when the brothers didn't do the big entrance whenever they visited one of their establishments. Did they slip through the back door?

If Nico is there too, maybe I could ask him for some cash or something. Make up a story about an angry landlord trying to kick me out or whatever. I could really, really use his infatuation with me for my benefit right now.

My skin starts itching just thinking about the great sensation of filling my bloodstream with the glorious white powder. I wipe my sweaty palms on my black skinny jeans, and before I talk myself out of it, grab a glass and fill it with the best Scotch we have.

Trying to look confident, I strut toward the double doors and glance up at the no-neck guard, who looks down at me as if I'm an annoying pest.

"Hi, uh, they called for me to bring a drink to the back."

The man crosses his arms and booms in a deep voice. "Boss told me to not let anybody in."

"Well, he must've changed his mind then," I sass, and flip my hair over my shoulder, trying to look taller, which is laughable with my unimpressive height.

He lifts an eyebrow but moves to the side with a muttered, "Whatever."

I try not to stumble and spill the drink in my rush to get past him, and only allow myself to breathe when the doors close behind me, cutting off the sounds of the club.

There's a small corridor in this part of the building with three doors on the right. The first door leads to Sergio's office, and right now, I hear two murmuring voices coming from the slightly ajar door.

I take a quick peek inside and see him talking to a guy I've never seen before, their faces unhappy. No sight of Nico, though. I retreat and try the other door. It's semi-dark, with only a few monitors from the surveillance cameras illuminating the area. Taking a quick sweep around the place tells me what I already kind of guessed before – there's no sign of Nico.

I'm almost out of the room when a sound of sniffling gets my attention, and I freeze. What was that?

I crane my neck back to check the corridor and, assured that no one detected me yet, step inside to close the door slowly. I turn on the light and blink a few times to adjust my eyes to the sudden brightness.

The first thing that gets my attention is the gun on a table by the wall that's furthest from me. Then, a jolt of excitement runs through me when I spot about a dozen little plastic bags filled with white powder right next to the weapon.

Would they know if I took just a bit from each one?

There's no time to think it through; the need to charge myself with the chemicals stronger than any reasonable thought. God, I'm turning into Christy.

I step to the table and grab the little zip lock bag with a shaking hand, and then almost cough up my heart in shock when something stirs by my leg.

I jump away and drop to see under the table, feeling my eyes almost pop out of my skull.

The wide, frightened eyes of a little girl stare back at me. Her mouth is gagged, and her hands are tied behind her back to the leg of the table with a hose tie. Tears stream down her blotchy face, and it takes everything in me not to pass out of the shock I feel at having this image right in front of me.

What the fuck is going on here?

My thoughts go back to Ramirez, and his malicious eyes, and I immediately snap to action.

Crouching in front of the girl, I frantically whisper, "I'll take this off, but you need to promise you will stay quiet and listen to everything I say, okay?"

Jesus Christ, I can't believe I'm doing this. Today is the day. I'm going to die, and surprisingly not by my own hands this time. They'll kill me when they get back and see me here trying to rescue this poor child. I want to giggle nervously as I take off the gag from the girl's little mouth and look for something to cut the ties with, thinking about how different it feels to actually fear death for once.

"What's your name?" I whisper after I find a cable cutter in one of the drawers under the glowing monitors.

"Nora," she breathes, her lips wobbling as if she's on the verge of melting.

"Okay, Nora, listen to me," I snap the ties and help her to her feet. "There's no time to waste here; I need to get you out of here. When we leave this room, you need to be as quiet as you can, and when I tell you to run, you run with everything you have, okay?"

She gives me a small nod, and I know that's the best I can get.

"Holy hell," I look at the ceiling, swallowing the oncoming tremor. I don't want to think too much about the repercussions of what I'm about to do, but it's coming at me regardless.

I glance at the surveillance system and see that there are cameras everywhere. There will be no point in pretending that it wasn't me after I walk out of this room with Nora. The brothers will surely find me and make me pay for stealing from them.

Stealing a human. A child. I can't stop the manic giggle from getting out this time.

When I glance back at the trembling little girl clinging to my pants, my mind is made up, however. I'm doing it, and if I die in the process of doing something good in my life, something right for once, then so be it.

I'm starting to turn toward the door when the sight of the drugs pulls me back in the direction of the table, and on an impulse, I grab what, I hope, is cocaine and stuff the gun in the back of my pants, hoping that it won't shoot my ass off accidentally. I grab the girl's wrist firmly and give her a look. She looks spooked, but there's also a strong determination and understanding in her gaze that should never grace the face of a child so young.

Since there were only three doors in the corridor, I assumed the last must be the exit door, and I closed my eyes briefly when the night breeze hit my face as soon as I opened it.

One last glance behind me, and the next thing I know, I'm running with Nora by my side for what feels like forever. I know it's only been about fifteen minutes when we reached my apartment complex, but in my mind, it's been a lifetime. Every heartbeat asking if it's going to be the last. Yet, there's no one behind me when I turn. The street is quiet, with barely any lights still on at some apartments.

My grandpa used to say that only harlots and thieves walk outside at an ungodly hour. He would probably say I'm both right now and shake his head with disappointment.

I never told anyone where we live, so I think it's safe to bring the girl here until I can think of a plan. The place is loud when we step into the apartment, and I glare at the switched-on TV set and playing radio when Nora whimpers in fright at the ear-assaulting sounds.

Christy must've left everything on again and went out. I grab the remote and turn it off before silencing the radio.

"Nora, are you... ?" I turn to address the kid when Christy comes out of her bedroom.

"What the fuck, Claire? I was listening to that!" With the way she stumbles, I can tell she's already taken whatever it is she's on these days, but it doesn't stop her from noticing the little girl in the middle of the room, looking ready to hide.

"Who's that?"

"Christy, before they kicked you out, did you tell anyone where we live?" I come to her and shake her arm until I'm able to redirect her attention to me.

"Are you nuts? Why would I do that? To get fucking creeps on our doorstep? Fucking idiot."

"No, Chris. I mean anyone from the staff. The boss, the girls, the bouncers, anyone..."

Her bloodshot eyes roll over my face with a sneer before glancing toward Nora.

"What did you do? Why aren't you at work?"

"I quit," I say and bite my lip, waiting for her reaction.

"You quit?" She asks slowly, her eyes tightening into tiny slits. "The fuck is wrong with you, Claire? Did you kidnap this little girl too? What is this, some fucking manic episode of your crazy ass or some shit?"

I ignore her remark about being crazy and tell her a short version of what happened.

Christy visibly calms down, but I know she's not happy with what I've pulled. With a shake of her head, she throws, "You better clean up if she makes a mess, Claire," and slams the door on her way out.

"Okay, Nora. You're probably hungry, huh? Maybe I could make you a snack, and you can tell me a little about yourself?" I step from foot to foot, suddenly feeling very inadequate to take care of a child even for a while. I'm so out of my element.

I've been an only child and never spent time with any kids, so I have no idea what to expect. Is she going to cry? Scream? Curse me?

But Nora only nods slowly before following me into the kitchen.

If the situation were any different, I would blush at the state I find the area in, but Nora doesn't seem to mind as she moves the empty takeout boxes from the chair and sits down before looking at me expectantly.

I turn on our rusty oven and set it to the right temperature before I fish out a frozen pizza from the fridge. The adrenaline that was cursing through me just a minute ago started to wear off, and I felt lightheaded and on the verge of tears.

My mind starts racing as I stare at the tiny timer above the oven.

What happened to Nora's parents, and why was she tied and hidden in the back room of the goddamn strip club? I know Sergio isn't an outstanding citizen waiting to do charity work in Chicago. But to kidnap a little girl?

I feel sick, knowing that I've been working for them for close to three years now, oblivious to what may be happening behind closed doors. What if I've been happily getting high and pouring drinks just as some other little girl was being locked there?

The timer dings, making me jump, and I grab the mitten to retrieve the steaming pizza with shaking arms. I cut it into triangles and place it in front of Nora.

I'm worried she'll burn her mouth when she grabs the first piece and bites into it eagerly, but she doesn't seem to care. The next piece is gone before I can even voice my worry about her getting sick from eating too much. There goes my hope about her only being captured for a few hours. She looks like it's been days since she last ate. The poor child is starving.

When she's on her third piece, her movements slow, and I chose this moment to question her a bit.

"Nora, where are your parents?" I sit opposite her slowly and wait for an answer.

Sadness pulls at her face for a fraction of a second before it's gone, and then she replies in a monotone voice, "Dead."

"Both of them?" I need to clarify, and she nods without meeting my gaze.

"How old are you?" Is my next question.

"Nine," she responds and reaches for the glass of water I placed in front of her before.

"Why were you at the club?" I'm scared to get the answer, but I need to know what happened. I have to know just how messed up the situation I got myself into is.

"They took me," she says, barely audible, and drops the uneaten pizza onto the plate, looking ashen.

"Took you from where?" I lean toward her and hesitantly reach my hand toward her, careful not to spook her. When she doesn't answer, I press, "I'm sorry if this is painful, Nora. But I need to know. So I can help you."

"They came to the house and screamed at my dad. Then they started to look for money. They destroyed everything, even my dollhouse. The man smashed it to pieces, and I started to cry. My mommy told me to be quiet, but I couldn't stop... The black devil told the big men to take me instead of the money. I didn't want to go... My dad was screaming, and then..."

Tears spill down from Nora's eyes, a look of absolute devastation taking over her innocent face, and she shuts her mouth tight. I slump in my seat, feeling drained and knowing this is so out of my depth.

I'll be taking Nora to the closest police station in the morning as soon as I'm packed and ready to leave. I know I'm done here in Chicago; the moment I go to the police and point fingers at the Ramirez brothers, it will be the same as signing my own death sentence. I know in my heart that they will hunt me for it until they put me down.

I've watched many movies and heard many stories. I know what happens to the snitches.

I excuse myself from the room, leaving Nora alone like a coward, and step into my room, where I throw the gun on the mattress and retrieve one of the zip lock bags from my pocket. Making a beeline to the small bedside table, I sprinkle the surface with the white stuff and make untidy thick lines with my finger before I breathe them into my system.

Right away, I sense it's not cocaine. The feeling is also euphoric, but something is off. My heart starts racing more than usual, and I have to squish the oncoming panic attack when the thought that I could be poisoned hits me.

When nothing of that sort happens within the next minute, I relax slightly, but the overwhelming feeling of paranoia doesn't seem to be going anywhere.

"Is this your room?" A small voice behind me calls, and I almost jump out of my skin.

"Hey! Nora!" I exclaim way too loudly, and the girl takes a frightened step back. "I'm, uh, I'm not feeling so swell right now. What'ya think 'bout getting some sleep?" I hear myself slurring my words more and more, but it's like I can't make my tongue to cooperate as I speak.

My thoughts seem clear, the whole world in focus, but somehow, my body didn't get the memo that I'm feeling so good and bright right now.

"You can take my bed while I pack and wait for my friend Christy to come back. I need to speak with her before we can go."

Nora eyes me like I've grown two heads but nods before taking a seat on my unmade bed. I can tell she's tired but tries to stay alert—poor kid.

I exit the room, trying to appear normal, but I know my moves are jittery at best. What the fuck is this shit? A rat poison?

After I splash some water on my face in the bathroom sink, I grab a plastic bag and throw essentials like a toothbrush and deodorant into it before walking back to the living room to take a look around.

I sigh in relief when I find Christy back in the apartment, sitting on the sofa while she munches on the pizza leftovers that Nora left in the kitchen, her eyes glued to the screen playing some kind of cooking show.

"Shit, Chris. I'm so glad you're here. Listen, I think I need to go away for a while... or maybe forever, I don't know. I- uh, shit, I fucked up. I know you probably don't approve, but I think I need to go to the police... Are you even listening to me?" I slap her arm when she doesn't acknowledge me and then watch a cruel smile grow on her face.

"Don't bother, Claire." Her eyes finally meet mine, and I don't like the look on her face.

"Don't bother what?"

"Don't bother rambling on about it. They're already on the way," she informs me with satisfaction.

"Who's on the way?" A shiver causes me to stumble over the question.

"The right owners of that little brat you brought," she informs me, to my horror and laughs.

"What did you do, Christy?"

"Saw a window of opportunity and used it to my advantage, obviously," she answers coldly, looking more sober and put together than I ever saw her this year. "They will surely pay me a pretty penny for helping them out. Maybe even give me back my job at the club, who knows?"

I stand to my feet and stare at her in shock before snapping my head toward the door when the screech of tires from outside reaches us.

"Oh, I know that look on your face. Little Claire is once again starting something that she can't fucking finish. You think you're so special, so cute, so fucking virginal. Look at me, I'm Miss Pristine. I'm so different and cool, yet I don't possess an ounce of backbone in my body to ever fight for what I deem worthy of my love and attention. All I can do is run, run, run..."

I tune out the mocking voice of the person that I considered almost family for years and do just as she says. Run.

Turning on my heel, I drop the bag with the toiletries and speed toward my bedroom, where I find Nora still sitting where I left her, staring blankly at the wall.

"We need to go right now!" I bark at her, making her flinch. I don't have time to feel bad about it, though; the sounds of a fist pounding on the door making me almost frantic. I grab Nora's arm and the gun and open the window. I push her through it first and then climb after her, stopping short when I come face to face with Nico.

"Claire, baby... what are you doing?" He grabs Nora's shoulder and holds her in place when she tries to run. I hear Sergio's voice coming from the inside of the apartment, asking where I am, and I see Nico open his mouth to call for him.

"Please, Nico, I didn't mean to stir anything. I just got scared... You don't have to do this. You know I always liked you..."

He shakes his head with a grimace, "I'm sorry, Claire, but I can't..."

"Then I'm sorry too," I cut him off before I lift the gun and pull the trigger, aiming for his foot, the one that is further away from screeching Nora.

I never used a gun before, so the force of the blast took me by surprise, making my aim a bit off, and I ended up shooting him in his thigh.

"You fucking bitch!" He roars and falls to the ground.

"Are you okay? Did I hit you?" I rush to Nora and check her body, aware that we'll be having more company in the next second.

She shakes her head no, so with a strength I didn't know I possessed, I lift her up and run as fast as I can. I hear a male shouting in the distance before the wheezing sound of bullets flying around me makes me stumble a bit. Determined to get us out of here and still operating on the unknown fuel I snorted; mixed with a shot of pure adrenaline, I sprint even faster.

When I see a bus pulling to a stop in my proximity, I switch directions and jump on board just as the driver starts closing the doors. I make Nora hide under the seat and bend my own head so we're not visible to whoever might be looking for us on the street.

I don't let myself relax, though. I know this is only the beginning.

CHAPTER XIII

SINCE I DIDN'T HAVE time to take anything of use besides the gun that I already dropped in the first bushes I saw as soon we exited the bus, I decided to work with what I had, which was the narcotics stuffed inside my pocket.

Going to my dealer's house was risky at best. After all, Christy is his regular customer, too, but I don't think I have a choice. We need money. At least enough to get us out of Chicago and to last us the few days I need to work out what to do.

I'm the least emotionally equipped person to do all this, and there's a big part of me that keeps whispering in my head to just give up. But every time I look at little Nora clutching at me and staring at me as if I'm her last lifeline – because I probably am, I feel a small sense of pride.

I'm doing the right thing. Wasn't being needed what I always wanted? Didn't I want to be brave like my best friend Jenny? Now is my chance.

The guy who usually sells to me goes by the nickname Rant, and I think it fits him very well because he is the biggest grump I ever met. To say he wasn't happy with the fact I came knocking so early in the morning would be an understatement. His girlfriend, Misty, who looks halfway dead already, was more than eager to try the new stuff I came with after I exaggeratedly told a story about the greatest high I had.

To my relief, she approved, and Rant was prone to pay me a hundred for it. I laughed in his face and managed to negotiate two hundred. It was still laughable, but time was not on my side, and he was getting agitated.

Nora witnessed the whole thing, unfortunately, and I wish I could spare her more trauma by not coming to a drug dealer's lair. But considering that she probably watched her parents being murdered before getting kidnapped and then being shot at not even an hour ago, I assume she's most likely numb to all of this. I know I am. Or maybe it's just the drugs wearing off.

I tap the half-empty baggy in my pocket to check if it's there and grab Nora's hand as we walk toward the bus station. I'm looking over my shoulder way too frequently, and I probably look suspicious as hell, dragging the dirty, disheveled girl behind me, but no one even spares us a glance. The sun is barely up, and most people wandering around are half-asleep, rushing to get to work.

The station is busy when we get there, the strong smell of fumes and tires making me gag. Sweat runs down between my shoulder blades when I look between the ticket office and the entrance to the public restrooms.

Again, my addiction wins, and I prowl through the crowd with Nora, barely keeping up with my stride. I don't care. It's sad, but I need it, even if I hate myself more and more with each step.

I tell her to wait by the sinks and almost fall into the stall, barely caring about closing the door to the disgusting-looking toilet. I shake out the contents of the small plastic packaging onto the top of my hand and inelegantly sniff it with a loud snort.

This time around, it's as if someone electrocuted me. I see everything turn brighter, the sounds coming from the station getting more distinct. But at the same time, everything seems to be further away and intangible.

There's not much left of my remedy, but I carefully roll the plastic and hide it in my pocket.

When I leave, my eyes go to the sink, and my knees almost buckle when I find the space empty.

"Nora? Nora!" I cry just as the stall next to mine opens, and the little head peeks through.

"I had to pee," she says quietly and goes to wash her hands.

I slap my hand on my wildly beating heart and try to stop my erratic breathing. This right here only proves that I am the last person on Earth who should take care of a child.

Jesus Christ, what if Ramirez followed us and used the first moment I lost sight of her? Shit, Claire. Focus. Focus, focus, focus.

Nora finishes and wipes her wet hands on her dirty pants before looking at me expectantly, seemingly oblivious to my freak-out.

"Come on," I grab her hand and quickly walk toward the ticket office, high and out of my mind.

"Two tickets to Madison, please," I almost yell to the clerk before I can even think it through, and then rush us toward the indicated terminal to board the already waiting stinky bus.

Just to be on the safe side, I move my back to the window and order Nora to duck until we're not passing through the freeway and leaving Chicago behind us.

Great, and now what?

I HAVE ONLY EVER BEEN to a few times to Madison, not counting my time at the hospital, but I can navigate through the city fairly well. It wasn't that hard to find a motel room that I could afford.

Nora dropped on the bed as soon as we entered the room and fell asleep about a second after I told her it was safe now to do so.

I, on the other hand, am not so lucky. It's been three hours since I've been pacing the short length of the room, too wired to get some rest.

We can't go to Bell Ridge. My father moved away soon after I tried to off myself, supposedly unable to live at the house any longer. And that's it for the people that could be of help.

But maybe... No, it's been too long, and I didn't keep tabs on what happened after I left. The whole town could be gone by now, and I wouldn't know any better.

Then, an idea struck me. Brody wasn't actually Bell Ridge; he turned out to be FBI. If there's a person more suitable to deal with this stuff, it's him. Yes! He would be perfect. I hope he remembers me.

How do I find him, though? Isn't the FBI in Washington? Or is that just in the movies? Can you just call them and ask for an agent you know?

"Nah, Claire, that's fucking stupid," I reprimand myself and then wince, worried that I woke Nora. When she doesn't even stir, I resume my pacing.

There has to be another way than going straight to the police. I don't trust anyone right now. What if Ramirez has someone in his pocket? What if I get there, and it makes everything even worse? What if they assume I kidnapped her? Would they believe my story?

I could really use my phone right now and do some online research on the stuff, but of course, all I have right now is about ninety dollars, sticky clothes damp from sweat on my back, and a traumatized kid in my care.

Eyeing Nora, I decide it's best to let her sleep and leave the room to speak with the pimply teenager sitting at the front desk of the motel to let me use the computer.

It takes some convincing and a big chunk of my barely existing budget, but he agrees and gives me an hour before stating he's going on a break and to ring a bell on the console if someone comes.

Not wanting to waste any time, I google the name Damon Brody and am surprised by the abundance of online articles and references I get right away. I blink back the stingy tears when I find a report of what happened at the Mill about a year ago, my hand going to the picture of a more mature Jenny with her chin jutted out defiantly at the photographer as she's smoking outside a hospital.

"She... she made it," I whisper in awe, my heart almost bursting with real happiness. Not the fake, medical-induced one, but real, pure joy.

Clicking out of the page, I scroll some more to find out what happened to Brody and find a company named DB Constructions operating here in Madison as one of the upper searches under that name. Could that be him? Unlikely, but this is my only chance. There's no Jenny Wallace or Damon Brody on social media that matches them unless they moved far away and don't have a profile pic.

"Are you done?" The bored voice behind me asks, and without waiting for my answer, the teenager moves the chair back, indicating that my hour is up and I should bounce.

I quickly scribble the address of the company on a notepad, much to the young clerk's annoyance, and walk out of the small office.

When I go back to the room, Nora is sitting by the headboard with her arms around her knees, flinching slightly when the door closes after me.

"Hey, I hope you didn't get scared when you saw me gone. I was just downstairs to speak to the clerk. I think I can find someone that can help us. You wanna come?"

The girl doesn't react, continuing to stare at the wall, but I see her arms trembling slightly. I take a seat next to her and sniffle when my nose starts burning.

I want to take her in my arms and console her, but I don't think it's me that she needs right now. She needs her parents and is probably just realizing that they won't be coming back. Ever. That her innocent life is over. And maybe that she's stuck with a mentally unstable junky as her last resort. Likely not; I think she's too young to think like that. Hopefully.

"Would you rather stay here and wait for me? I can bring you some snacks from the little store we passed while coming here. What do you like? Chocolate? Candy? Maybe some chips?"

Again, I don't get a reaction, and I sigh. "Okay, I get it. I'll be back as soon as I can, okay? Don't open the door for anyone else apart from me. Don't go out. Please just... Wait for me."

Nora blinks slowly, indicating that she heard me, so I stand to walk on unsteady legs toward the bathroom.

My reflection in the rectangular mirror above the sink causes me to wince. I look awful—no remnants of the sweet Claire I used to be. The purple bags under my eyes and the sheen of sweat coating my pale skin make me look sick. There's nothing else here than a bar of soap, so I use it to quickly wash as best as I can and then comb my tangled hair with my fingers. I try to straighten my clothes, but it's no use. They're too wrinkled and dirty.

Staring at my reflection brings a heavy wave of despair that almost suffocates me, and I have to grab onto the sink to keep myself from falling to the floor in a heap. I can't fucking do it. None of it.

I'm too weak. Too pathetic. Too unstable.

I wrap my hand around the small plastic bag in my pocket and hesitate. If I do this right now, I won't be getting more anytime soon, and I feel my body protesting at the thought. But if I don't charge myself a bit, I won't be brave enough to leave the motel and search for people who could help me.

At this point, my body takes over, and I lean over the flat surface next to the sink to quickly snort the small line. My body buzzes from the hit, and a wave of nausea pulls at my stomach. I don't know when was the last time I've eaten something, but whatever is occupying my stomach right now is desperate to get out. I breathe a few times through my nose, and something wet touches my lip.

A small trail of blood leaves one of my nostrils, and I groan. Shit.

Quickly, so my t-shirt doesn't get stained, I wash it off and wait for the nosebleed to pass before I check my reflection one more time. At least I've got more color on my face now.

I exit the bathroom and don't even glance at the small body curled up on the bed.

"I'll be back," I say stiffly and almost run out the door.

In a haze, I find a taxi and give him the address, ignoring the way he eyes me, and slump in the seat as the city landscape passes in front of my eyes. I wish the image felt more real because now I'm under the illusion everything looks like a part of a video game. The colors are blotchy and unshapely. I snap my head to the side when I hear a whisper right next to me and startle at the revelation that there's no one actually there.

Am I losing the last bits of my sanity? What kind of potion was Ramirez selling to people? I want to crawl out of my own skin. I want to heave. I want to...

"This is the place," the car comes to a stop on the other side of the street, and I take a look around, snapping out of the labyrinth of my mental hell for a moment.

"That'll be nine dollars," the driver says louder, looking over his shoulder, but I don't see him.

All I can focus on is the familiar big guy dressed in black, walking with a cane around a white, dusty pickup truck before he gets behind the wheel and drives off.

I can't believe it. Damon Brody. It's him. But why does he work in a construction company? I thought he was FBI. Shit. Maybe he can still help somehow. He knows people. I'm sure of it.

"Miss," the driver prompts impatiently, and I wave at the car that's pulling away in the other direction.

"Follow this car, please," I say to the driver, and he snorts.

"This isn't a movie. I'm not going to chase after a car. Pay the fare and get out."

"Did I tell you to chase him, or did I say follow him?" I snap at the man. "Just drive, goddamn it. No chasing."

My voice sounds off even to my own ears, and I wonder for a second if I appear as high as I am to everyone who encounters me, or is it just in my head?

The man shakes his head and grumbles under his breath but surprisingly moves the car and drives after Brody. His car is already turning right at the next intersection when we pull back onto the road, and we almost lose him for a second before I point the right car to the driver.

"Right there, turn here!"

"Fine! Jesus, no need to rip my eardrum to shreds. Fucking freak." He says the last part under his breath, but I still hear it. The phrase so often used by people to describe me.

When Brody turns toward a narrow, rocky road with a dead-end sign, I tell the driver to stop and pay for the fare with the last of my money.

God, I hope this is going to work.

I walk through the forest for what feels like forever until I come to a clearing and find a beautiful wooden cabin, Brody's car, parked in the driveway. There's no fence, so I walk straight to the door and ring the bell.

"Just a minute!" A voice of a woman calls from inside, and my breath hitches.

Is that... ?

CHAPTER XIV

"CLAIRE?" JENNY GASPS and takes a step back, looking at me as if she saw a ghost.

"I'm- I'm sorry for showing up like this, but I need your help," I stammer nervously and step from foot to foot. I still feel over-energized, but also the blow sharpened my anxiety and apprehension when it comes to standing in front of the person I lost. The one I probably disappointed the most, even more than I ever did myself.

Another tremor runs through me, and I have to grind my teeth not to let it show, but I needn't have to worry about it because Jenny launches at me, almost knocking me over. Her heavy sobs run through my body, and I wish I were more present to enjoy this moment without my mind being all over the place. I dreamt about this so many times, and I always thought I would be the one sobbing in relief. But here I am, doped out of my goddamn mind.

"Jen? Who is it?" I hear a concerned male voice before Brody steps into my line of sight and, similarly to Jenny before, takes a step back as if I'm some phantom coming to haunt him. "Oh, shit!"

Jenny steps away a little, close enough to still keep her hands on my shoulders but far enough to give me a quick once over. I can tell the second in which she notices that there's something wrong with me, other than my more than disheveled appearance, her intelligent eyes meeting mine briefly before I look to the side.

She sniffles loudly before touching my face tenderly like she used to when we were teenagers and I was having one of my meltdowns. "You're going to be okay, babe." Her low whisper meant to only reach my ears.

I hang my head in shame, feeling the positive effects of the drug wearing out a bit with her words. Tears start to flow freely down my twisted face, landing on Jenny's perfect house doorstep.

"Come on, it's chilly outside. Not that it's any better inside since the heater broke, but still..." She mutters as she grabs my hand and leads me into the cozy interior of the cabin.

I sit down on the plushy sofa, relishing in the soft feel of fabric under my palms, and sigh. This feels like heaven.

Quiet murmurs of the conversation between the couple resonate throughout the open plane of the first floor, but for the life of me, I can't concentrate on anything else other than the feeling of safety that the comfy seating provides for me right now.

The drugs are fleeting my body with each of my heartbeats. I can sense it as the anxiety, fear, and paranoia slowly enter my mind, making me want to burrow myself under the throw pillows or the soft sponge inside the sofa cushions.

Shit, my mind is warped.

I don't know how much time passes as I try to become one with Jenny's furniture, but when a door slams somewhere in the house, I jump to my feet as if burned and look around in alarm. I run to the window, sure to find Ramirez with his goons waiting outside for me.

But of course, after wildly looking around, I see that there's no one here other than Jenny, who's leaning on the wall and observing my behavior with passiveness I didn't know she was capable of.

"Where's the big guy gone?" I chirp as if trying to pretend that this is normal, and I didn't just come here high as a kite ten minutes ago after being gone for years.

"Brody went to fix the heater and then left for work," she says slowly, eyeing me. "You've been... out of it for an hour now."

An hour? What the...

"Shit. Nora..." I put my hand to my mouth, my eyes going wide. I was meant to be gone for a few minutes, but it's been... My eyes spring around, trying to find a clock before landing on a digital one placed on the small desk in the corner.

Fuck. It's been two hours.

"Oh, no," I grab my hair in panic and then whirl around to find Jenny standing close by. She grabs my arm, palpably done with my erratic behavior, and drags me back to sit.

"What did you take?" She asks in her no-nonsense tone.

"I don't know exactly," I mutter and draw invisible patterns on my legs, unable to look her in the eyes.

"Okay, how long ago was it?"

I scratch my head and blink a few times, trying to remember the time on the clock that I literally had in front of my eyes a second ago. Damn it, I need me some Coke right now.

I should've just stayed in the club, continued my work, and don't stick my nose into things that weren't my business. All would be fine.

"Who's Nora?" Jenny questions when I take too long to answer.

"That's a long story," I whisper.

"Well, I've got time, Claire. You told me you came here for help..."

I did?

"... but to achieve that, I need to know what is going on." She presses, and I can feel the sofa deepening as she sits next to me. "Let me help you."

I finally pull enough courage to meet her gaze, and some of my anxiety lets out right away when I see her expression.

This is my best friend right here. She doesn't look at me like I'm a freak, or a disappointment, or someone who should be pitied. No. Her eyes are full of compassion, understanding, and pain of her own.

Whatever I'm going through, she feels for me.

"I guess I just better show you. Do you have a car?"

"Yeah, but if you're taking me somewhere, I need to take Henry with us. I don't have anyone who'll babysit him on such a short notice."

"Who's Henry?" I frown at her.

And for the first time since I came to, Jenny's face lightens up, and she jumps to her feet and drags me with her.

"Come on, we'll splash you with some cold water. When was the last time you ate? You look worse than I did as a teenager."

"THIS IS YOUR KID?" I stand shyly to the side, my hair still wet from the cold shower Jenny threw me into. It wasn't exactly pleasant, but the freezing water and the strong coffee my friend pushed into my hands helped me gain some clarity.

"Yup," she smiles.

"He came out of you? Like... for real?" I question, my wide eyes on the cutest little boy with curly hair, just like Jenny's.

"Straight out of my vagina," she smirks and goes to stand in front of the kid who's yet to acknowledge our presence as he builds a complicated-looking structure from plastic elements.

"But how?" I can't wrap my head around it.

"Do you mean it as a technical question or more like a philosophic one?"

"Both?"

Jenny laughs and nudges the little boy with her foot to get his attention.

"What do you say we go on a little trip with Aunt Claire?"

"Okay," he replies simply, and without any further due puts his toys away and grabs the hand Jenny extends toward him, eyes bright and fully innocent.

The picture makes me want to cry, but I just smile at him when he gives me a scanning look that is too insightful to fit on his chubby little face.

"Are you sad?" He asks and doesn't wait for an answer. "Mommy was sad today."

Jenny grimaces and rubs her belly, revealing a small bump as the oversized t-shirt she's wearing flattens under her hand.

She either ate a large breakfast, or she's producing another human soon. And I don't understand why, but the thought makes me even more depressed.

"Can we go now? Because I already left Nora alone for too long." I address Jenny, remembering that I left the little girl like the irresponsible no-brain that I turned into.

"Sure, let's go. And you can start talking when we're on the road." Jenny throws me a challenging look, and I hang my head as I walk after her.

"Yeah, okay."

I'm scared of revealing just how bad things got after she had to run away from the little town we lived in. I'm scared to face all the things that I've done that led me toward this moment.

"YOU ACTUALLY SHOT HIM?" Jenny whispers from the driver's seat as she stops the car in a parking lot in front of the motel I left Nora at. Then she glances in the mirror to check if her son is still busy with the little device she handed him before to keep him occupied.

"I shot at him, and the bullet happened to find his thigh," I state confidently, and Jenny chuckles.

"Damn, I missed you, Claire." She shakes her head, and then her smile disappears when she remembers why we're here.

In silence, we exit the car, and I wait on the side while Jenny unstraps Henry from the car seat.

Each step on the stairway brings me more fear, and I want to turn around.

What if Sergio already knows we're here, and I am leading my best friend into a trap? What if Nora didn't listen to me and escaped and is now wandering around the unfamiliar streets of Madison on her own?

A hand touches my shoulder, and I glance behind me at Jenny. She gives me a gentle smile, but her eyes are determined. I give her a nod and then walk toward the door to the room I rented.

"Nora?" I call out to the half-dark room before I step in. As soon as my eyes adjust, I notice her, and all the air leaves my lungs in a loud whoosh.

Everything in the room looks just as I left it.

"Okay, I gotta ask. What exactly was your plan? Just take her and keep her in a motel room?"

"I have no idea. Everything happened so fast, Jenny. It was an impulse. I didn't think it through, obviously, but I know they're searching for us. The only thing on my mind was getting her out of there."

Jenny stares at the little girl who's sitting curled up in the armchair in front of the outdated TV box. Nora's posture is stiff, and I can see that she's only pretending to watch the show that's on as she monitors everything we say and do.

"Shit. What about the police?" She bites her lip and lets go of her son's hand when he tugs on it to get away. He casually strolls to the other armchair next to Nora and sits down. The girl flinches slightly and eyes him with silent interest before her eyes go back to the screen.

I sent Jenny an "Are you fucking for real" look before quietly saying, "I thought you would be the last person in the world to ever trust the police."

"My father was a dirty cop, and there are plenty of those fuckers, but Brody knows a few decent ones here in Madison. I'm sure he could contact someone..." she shrugs casually, but her face doesn't look as certain.

"I'm not sure, Jenny," I mumble and then lean to her ear so that the kids won't hear. "I'm not exactly an angel. I was on drugs, and... what if they charged me with like child endangerment or something? That's a thing, right?"

"Oh shit. I never even thought of that," she grabs the bridge of her nose and rubs it as if to get rid of a headache, then she straightens and puts her hands on her hips with a resigned sigh. "If Damon finds out, he's going to fucking flip."

"So... let's not tell him, yeah?" I say with a smile and flutter my eyelashes.

She rolls her eyes but smiles, too, despite the situation. "Shit, I never could say no to your cuteness. I'll tell you what. I will tell him, but he won't get the whole gruesome version, okay?"

"Yeah, okay," I nod, and then my eyes travel back to Nora.

"I think I may have an idea how to help her. But we will need to call for backup," Jenny says and fishes out her phone from a purse.

"WELL? WHAT DO YOU THINK?" Jenny asks the older woman named Ruth.

She glances at Nora and sighs. "Well, I can't accept a child into the shelter. It's against the rules..." She lifts a finger when my friend tries to interject. "However, I'm friendly with a few people from CPS. I'll call a woman named Dahlia, who helped me once with a somewhat similar case. Until then, the girl is welcome to stay with me and Frank."

"That would be great," Jenny breathes and then lowers her gaze to meet mine. "Right, Claire?"

I hug my middle and grimace. "I dunno. Shouldn't I be the one taking care of her? It's my mess."

"Excuse us, Aunt Ruth," she addresses the woman standing on her right and then nods to the one called Amelia, who came with the older woman. They both look nice, and I trust Jenny, but I don't exactly feel right about pushing Nora into someone else's arms.

"We'll be back in a second."

"We'll keep an eye on them. Take your time," Amelia says and puts a hand on Henry's head.

Jenny walks out of the motel room and descends from the stairs, not waiting for me.

When I reach her, she pins me with a serious stare.

"Claire, I know your heart is in the right place since you've risked so much to rescue that poor girl. But, babe, you're not in a position to help anyone right now. Look at you," she waves her hand up and down, and I wince as if I received a physical blow. "You need help. You need to stop taking that shit, and you need to find yourself. I'm happy that you came to my door, Claire. More than that. I'm fucking ecstatic. But right now, you're just a shadow of the person that I know is inside there," this time, she jabs a finger right above my breastbone.

"I'm... I-I don't know how to do that..." I say brokenly. "Even right now, the bigger part of my brain is screaming for me to find a dealer. I want to get high so bad. You know there's never a bad day or a bad feeling. The anger that always sneaks up on me from nowhere. The devastation. The fucking... mania. It's just gone. And I fucking love it, Jenny."

She grabs my hands and dips her head to catch my eyes. "I know, Claire. I've been where you are. It felt so good. But I fucking hated myself more and more with each day. This is all just a ruse; the feeling of euphoria is not real, you know it. You're not getting rid of the sadness, and you're just burying it deeper and letting it fester."

"So, how do I stop?"

"If you're unable to do that for yourself, start by concentrating on the people you love. The people who depend on you."

"I've been alone for so long," I cry, my legs almost giving up on me under the invisible force of that statement. The heavy feeling of loneliness squashed me under its weight.

Jenny pulls me into her embrace and rocks us both from side to side with a shushing sound.

"I love you. I'm not going to leave you alone with this. Whatever comes our way, we will deal with this together."

"What if we're ripped apart again? I can't go through that again, Jenny. The last time destroyed me. I can't do this again; I won't survive another loss." I'm basically babbling hysterically at this point, but Jenny just continues to swing us slowly and then begins to rub my back.

"We're not powerless kids anymore, Claire. Things have changed for the better. Do I still have nightmares and am tortured by the past? Yes. But I also know that I'm stronger than I used to be. And if you aren't feeling strong right now, then let me lift some of that weight for you for a while. I promise you, you're not alone."

"Thank you," I mutter and tilt my head back before I leave slobber on Jenny's shoulder. Grabbing the edge of my sweatshirt, I wipe my runny nose and laugh at her disgusted face.

"You're so gross, dude," she laughs, but then it transforms into one of her soft smiles. "Come on, let's go back up to deal with the urgent stuff. When we get back home, we'll talk about the detox you'll have to undergo."

"Yeah, okay," I say lightly, but at the same time can't stop the shudder that runs through my body at the thought.

I haven't had a day without pumping my blood with anything for years.

And I know giving it up is going to suck so, so bad.

Oh, God, please help me get through it without killing myself.

CHAPTER XV

AIDAN - THREE MONTHS later

Brody parks the company pickup truck next to a wooden house, and we all exit to see it from close. I stand next to Tommy, a guy who's been working for the boss for a while now, whom I've become good friends with practically over the first week I started.

It came as a surprise that I would find a connection with the quiet, kind type, but Tommy has been fucked over by life a lot, so maybe that's how we were able to bond so fast. We've both been through it, but in entirely different ways. Yet, the unspoken understanding we share made it possible for us to become each other's rock. He helped me a lot during the hard transition I had to undergo when I came out of prison—no judgment – just kindness.

And having him teach me the ropes about working on a construction was a great bonus. I found out very soon how pedantic Brody can be when it comes to his projects and how badly he reacts when you fuck something up. And I did fuck up a lot of stuff at first. But I'm proud to say that those rookie mistakes are few and far between now.

"Another project?" I ask Tommy under my breath and glance at the woodsy yet modern construction.

Tommy just shrugs and walks after the boss as he continues to limp around the house without his cane, waving his hands around as he discusses something with his uncle who came with us today.

The old man is named Frank, and he sometimes shows up to fill in for Brody when he's dealing with some "family issues". I actually like those days, not because we don't have to work as hard as we do, but because it's still hard for me to be in the man's presence and not be reminded of what I did and about my time in prison.

When we round the house, I catch sight of a big ass terrace facing the forest and a small garden with flowerbeds and neatly trimmed bushes. Tommy joins them, and they all start to discuss something, but since I'm still only the helper, I don't bother joining.

All of a sudden, Brody turns around and addresses me as Tommy comes back to stand by my side.

"So, what you think?"

"About... ?"

"About the house."

I glance at it once more. "Um, nice digs, I guess?"

He gives me a deadpan stare as his uncle makes a weird sound and then coughs, trying to cover it. I don't know if it was a sound of disapproval or if he's amused by my dumbass act.

Tommy jabs me with his elbow and whispers, "Dude, that's the boss's house."

"Oh? Oh! Yeah, man, nice house. I like the..." I wave my hand around, indicating the whole building. My God, why can't I be normal around the man that signs my fucking paychecks and my goddamn parole papers.

"That's not what I meant," he grinds, and I can see he's truly annoyed. And in a terrible mood today. Before he can continue, Frank cuts in.

"We were talking about reconstructing the house since it's going to be tight in there soon with the new baby coming."

"Oh, shit. You're having a baby? That's great, man. Congrats!" I say sincerely, kind of surprised by the news. I don't know much about Brody's personal life, and I never ask, not even Tommy. Brody and I aren't friends, no matter how much time we spend working together. I just owe him.

For the first time since he pulled up to grab us this morning, Brody's lips turn up in a smile. "Thanks." Then he looks up at the house, and his expression quickly turns back to the stony one. "There's not a chance we will finish before she's born, but I guess we'll just put the crib in our bedroom for a few months."

"You know it would be easier to accommodate you all if your guest moved to the shelter like Ruth offered," Frank mutters to him, but his eyes are glued to the house.

Brody shakes his head and sighs, "Jen doesn't want to even hear about it. It's like they're fucking joined at the hip. She's watching her like a hawk all the time, worried that she'll relapse." The last part is said quieter, and I don't know if it's so Tommy and I don't hear it, or he just doesn't want whoever's in that house to know his thoughts on the subject.

Frank murmurs something back and then shakes his head before snapping his eyes to me.

"So, can you do it, kid?"

"What exactly do you want me to do here?" I ask, confused.

"You can draw, right? And Tommy here told us that you've been thinking about starting that online architecture course and whatnot. Maybe you'll come up with an idea of rebuilding the house so it doesn't look wonky when we finish but has enough space to fit the whole family."

I actually started the classes two months ago. But I won't voice that.

After getting my GED diploma while in prison, I struggled with finding the motivation to pursue getting an actual degree even when there were free courses available for us. I thought there was no way I'd be out so soon, so I gave up on further education.

A few weeks of living out in the real world again opened my eyes. I wouldn't say I'll be starving anytime soon, but man, do I have an epiphany when it comes to the hardships of living on my own. Growing up, I never swam in money, but Saint always provided everything I needed after I came to live with him. Sure, I had to work for him, but it wasn't the same.

Working on the construction sites and watching the architects work on the side gave me an idea. So, I called my parole officer, Sandra, to ask if it's even possible for a person on parole to get some funds to study. Two days later, she called me to say that she got me into some kind of rehabilitation education program for ex-convicts, and they happened to do courses on architecture and design.

However, I was not ready to share the news with people other than Tommy in case I turned out to be horrible at it and failed.

I glare at him now and throw under my breath, "Blabbermouth." To which he winces and lowers his head, looking like a timid little boy.

To Brody and Frank, I say, "Look, yeah, I can draw, but I'm not an architect. I don't know if I would be any good at it..."

The old man claps his hands as if it's settled and grins. "A perfect way to practice and learn then. I'll tell ya, boy, the school is one thing, but life experience is more valuable than that. Think of how much easier it will be for you if you already have one project under your belt."

Brody rubs at his face as I mull it over and then lifts his head to look at me. "Look, Aidan, we're not swimming in cash here by any means. I could do it myself, like when I was first building it to save money. But I just don't have the fucking time or patience, and... I'm getting too fucking old, I guess. Not to mention my fucked up leg. You can draw, and I know you're creative as fuck and resourceful when needed to be. I'm willing to trust that you can come up with something good. Then you and Tommy can work on it together after your regular shift to earn extra money. It can be a good chance for you to prove yourself, just as Frank said."

"Uh, when you put it that way... I can't really say no," I scratch at my head and look at the house through a new set of eyes. Right away, an idea enters my mind, and I smile at the two men looking at me expectantly. "All right, I think I can come up with a few ideas."

Brody nods his head, seemingly satisfied with my answer. "Glad to hear it. Tomorrow, I'll give you the plans of the house so you can have the full picture. But if you want to take a look inside to see if it sparks something, we can go in. The girls are out from what I know."

"Yeah, okay," I agree and follow him and Frank as they walk back toward the front yard.

Tommy quickens his steps, so we walk shoulder to shoulder. "Sorry about that. I didn't think."

I punch his arm but smile. "We're cool."

"Okay," he replies softly, clearly relieved.

We just round the corner of the house when a car pulls up into the driveway.

"Guess we'll be taking a rain check on the house tour," Brody throws over his shoulder, his expression light and happy before he walks to greet the obviously pregnant young woman, who exits the driver's side. Her wild, curly hair waves in the wind as she steps on her tippy-toes to kiss him.

Then she looks down and glares. "Where's your stick?"

Brody leans toward her ear to whisper something, and she snorts loudly before rolling her eyes.

He moves back with a grin, and it's then that my attention snaps to the movement on the other side of the car.

I see the top of a blonde head before it disappears by the back passenger door. Not even a minute later, a small boy rounds the vehicle to run straight at Frank.

"Uncle Frank!" He squeals happily and jumps up and down with a wide smile, revealing a wide gap of a missing tooth.

"And what am I? Thin air?" Brody teases from behind him, and the boy twirls around, forgetting the old man, as he quickly slams into his father's legs.

"Daddy! Aunt Claire bought me an ice cream cone, but she told me it's gonna be our secret," he tattles.

Until that point, me and Tommy were standing awkwardly to the side, watching the family scene unfold, uncertain what to do with ourselves, but at the mention of the name, my whole body turned on alert.

It couldn't possibly be her, right? I mean, what are the odds?

Soon enough, I get my answer when the person rummaging in the trunk rounds the car with hands full of plastic bags. And the time literally stops. In one millisecond, I drink her sight from bottom to top, trying to absorb everything as if afraid that she's just a product of my imagination that will disintegrate as soon as I blink.

Claire gives Brody her trademark sweet smile and then laughs. The sound makes my chest hurt, and I rub at the place to stop the burning sensation.

"And you have no idea what a secret means, right?" She asks the little guy, to which he shakes his head, but his smile is mischievous.

"Here, let me help you carry the stuff, girlie," Frank reaches out his arms, but Claire just shakes her head and sidesteps him.

"Nah, I got it. I'll just..." our eyes meet, and she stills as if she slammed into an invisible wall.

Her skin turns even paler than it was, to the point that her lips turn almost purple. And I can see them moving slightly as she mouths my name.

Then, a few emotions run through her face. The initial look of shock transforms into a look of longing that slowly turns into a deep sadness, only to end up with anger mixed with resentment.

She lifts her chin as if to dare me to say anything before she marches into the house without a word.

I unglue my eyes from the door and remember that we have company. I'm scared to look at others, but breathe out in relief when I see that Brody and Frank are laughing at something the little boy said.

But then I feel burning on the side of my face, and I snap my gaze at the other woman and gulp at the way she eyes me.

The hand that I was still holding on my chest falls limply to my side before I turn, almost falling into a puzzled-looking Tommy on my way to get back in the truck.

Before I can close the door to hyperventilate in peace, Tommy gets in after me, forcing me to scoot over.

"What happened? Are you sick? You look like you're going to throw up, man. And the boss will snap you in half if you do that here."

"That was Claire," I wheeze and bang my head on the headrest.

"Claire?" Tommy questions in confusion and then whips his head toward the house before looking at me with wide eyes. "As in the Claire? Your Claire?" He almost yells, and I have to fight the desire to punch him in the face so he'll keep it down.

"Oh, yeah, I guess she did look familiar," he muses.

Sometimes, Tommy and I hang around at my place, and the first time he came, he got interested in my drawings and who's the mysterious girl that features most of them. Since I was already four beers in, I broke and told him the whole story. Crying and raging like a bitch. We haven't talked about it since, but I guess he didn't forget my meltdown over the woman who seemed to be living in my boss's house.

"Man, you're fucked," Tommy says after a minute of silence.

"Yeah," I sigh. After the look I received from Claire's friend, there's no doubt in my mind that my days working for Brody are numbered.

We both sit straighter in our seats when the front doors open, Brody and Frank getting in with smiles on their faces.

"Okay, let's get back to work," Brody says, glancing at us through the rearview mirror before he backs out of the driveway.

I throw Tommy a look, and he nods with a silent promise not to tell anything.

I relax slightly and glance at the passing landscape, not really seeing anything other than the look on Claire's face when she saw me.

And then I go back to the details of her appearance. She looked much skinnier than should be considered healthy, her skin almost translucent under the sunlight. Even when she smiled at the boy, her smile never reached her eyes. Claire will always be the most beautiful girl for me, but today she looked... I don't know, like she was withering away or something.

My stupid worry over the job and my parole goes out the window as a new set of nerves settles in my sternum.

"... watching her like a hawk all the time, worried that she'll relapse..."

Was he talking about Claire? Relapse of what? Is she ill?

If I'm not fired by tomorrow, I'll give it a chance of getting closer and maybe finding out what is going on. I need to know if my girl is okay. And yes, in my mind, she will always belong to me. Now, after seeing her in the flesh, as opposed to just my dreams, I can say with confidence that my love for her is still very much alive, the same way it was all those years ago.

And with that, a new feeling of determination enters my brain, and I know I don't care about anything else in my life other than her well-being and making sure she's happy.

Even if Brody fires my ass, I will still be there to make things right and cater to her every need.

Yes, I fucked up. And some could say that should be the end of the story. But I paid the price. I did my time, and now my head is straight. There are no more secrets weighing me down. There's nothing left to hide.

I just pray that it will be enough. That not all is lost. That somehow I can still fix this.

CHAPTER XVI

I TRY TO SHIELD MY body with Tommy's as we stand in front of Brody's door, which is ridiculous because he's shorter. But I'm actually scared to walk into that house.

I've already created a few drafts of the outside of the house with the added space, but I can't put away coming inside any longer. I hold my big folder in front of me like a shield and gulp when the door opens, revealing the tall, curly-haired woman.

She smiles warmly at Tommy as she opens the door wider for us to come in.

"Hi guys, Brody mentioned that you may stop by today. Sorry about the mess," she winces, waving at the open space.

Usually, when someone makes a statement like that, they tend to exaggerate, but even I have to admit that the house is in total disarray. The sofa is spread out to make a bed with twisted blankets and pillows, making it look like whoever slept there had to be tossing and turning. Around it, there are loads of female clothes littering the floor, along with a few children's toys discarded in random places.

And when I get a look at the kitchen space... Wow, it's a mess.

She must see our reactions, although Tommy does a great job of looking passive because she adds with a sigh: "It's getting a little crowded in here."

"That's why I'm here," I say, stepping forward with my hand extended. "I'm Aidan Linden."

She grabs my hand and shakes it with surprising strength. "Oh. I know who you are."

The way she says it makes me wonder if there's a hidden meaning behind her words, but then she drops my hand and smiles.

"I'm Jennifer Wallace. Thanks for agreeing to help us."

"I still don't know how much of a help I will be... Wait. *Wallace*?" I make big eyes at her, and then a bulb goes off in my head. I literally have to stop myself from slapping my forehead. How the fuck I didn't put two and two together?

I'm so fucking stupid it's embarrassing. Brody's Jen is Jenny. *The* Jenny. Well, I guess it makes perfect sense now that Claire is here.

Jenny actually snorts at my shock. "I know, right? I'm somewhat of a celebrity in Bell Ridge. Unfortunately, not positively. But I'm just a regular girl in Madison, so who cares about that godforsaken town."

"And... you're okay with me being here? You know... After everything?" I eye her carefully, ready to get the fuck out of here if my presence is causing the pregnant woman any kind of stress.

"Brody deemed you worthy, and I trust his judgment. And I'm not an angel by any means. Did lots of stupid shit a few years back. I'm happy that people around me were able to look past that." She states matter-of-factly and then glances toward the staircase when her son calls for her.

"I'll be upstairs if you need me." She puts her foot on the first step and pauses before pinning me down with a freezing look, so at odds with her mellow attitude just from seconds ago. "Oh, and Aidan. Claire is not here right now and will be gone for a couple of hours. I don't know what's the deal between you two yet. But you better be gone by the time she comes back. Understand?"

"Yes, uh, I understand," I stammer out.

She looks pleased by my answer and continues to climb the stairs before disappearing upstairs.

I take a deep breath and then glance at Tommy, who's still looking at the top of the staircase.

"Dude. She's fucking terrifying. I would literally shit myself if she gave me that look."

"Yeah… I can see why she and boss make sense now," I mutter and open my clean binder. "We better get to it then. Take the measuring tape and start from this wall." I command, and together, we work in silence.

I try to ignore Claire's things that are in my way, fighting with the weird need to sniff her clothes or pillows like a total creeper.

"I'm sorry, man, but I gotta say this. Your girl is a total slob." Tommy says after a while, as he almost loses balance after tripping on some of the stuff lying around on the floor.

"Nah, man. She's just... Chaotic," I find myself replying as I continue to draw the space. "A beautiful chaos."

"Wow, you still got it bad," he laughs, and I lift my head up from my project to glare at him before snapping the binder shut.

"Come on, we have to get upstairs and finish before the time is up," I grumble.

Surprisingly, the second floor is in total contrast to the disarray downstairs. The door to the main bedroom is open, the door of the next room is slightly ajar, and I can hear Jenny's soft voice mixed with the murmurs of a little boy.

I enter the first room and almost snort at the meticulous way the bed is made, knowing that sometimes Brody's military background shines through his pedantic behaviors. The whole bedroom is spotless, and even the clothes in the open closet are neatly stacked.

Clearly, the chaos is kept outside this room.

I take a quick sketch of the room with the addition of extra space if we remodel the house structure and then motion with my head for Tommy to follow me.

I knock on the door to the kid's room, and when I'm told to enter, I step through the threshold only to stop short.

Jenny sits on the carpet with tears running down her cheeks, one of the toys squeezed tightly to her breasts. The boy doesn't pay her any mind as he continues to play and talk to his mom without waiting for any answer.

"Uh, is this a bad time?" I ask awkwardly, aware that Tommy leans over my shoulder to see what's going on.

She waves her hand dismissively and rolls her eyes. "Don't mind me. Just stupid pregnancy hormones." But the sad look in her tells me that it's actually more than that. My face must've shown my doubt because she sighed and glanced at her son. "Henry, baby, can you grab your toys and go downstairs to play for a bit? These nice men want to take a look around your room to make it better."

Henry eyes us both with interest before raising his hand in a small wave.

I grin at him and wave back before observing as he obediently stands up from the carpet, grabs two monster trucks in both hands, bends to kiss Jenny on the cheek, and then slides between me and Tommy to slowly descend the stairs.

I don't know much about kids. But that one is a bit weird.

When I turn my head, I see the woman trying to get to her feet, and I rush to give her a hand. She takes it gladly and then fixes her dress.

"Thanks," she mutters.

"Are you okay? Do you want me to call the boss?" I ask her, and she immediately gives me a look of displeasure.

"Don't you even dare. He's oversensitive enough as it is."

"All right?" I reply as she continues to cry, and I look to my friend for help. Tommy gives me a shrug and spreads his arms as if trying to ask, "What do you want me to do?"

"So, um, is the baby okay?" I ask awkwardly.

"Yeah, she's fine. I'm fine; everything is fucking fine." Jenny answers but swipes angrily at her wet face. "It's just that everything is a goddamn mess, you know?"

No. I don't know. I have no idea what is happening, actually. But I don't say that; instead, I question her gently. "Do you mean Claire? Is she, um... She looked sick the other day."

"Claire is... she's getting there. It's not easy watching her struggle, but-" Her eyes snap to me. "I guess I shouldn't really speak with you about that."

"Um. Probably not," I scratch at my head nervously. "So if it's not her, then why are you crying? If you don't mind me asking," I rush to say and glance at Tommy again, seeking guidance.

Jenny looks above my shoulder with her brows pulled down, her eyes unfocused.

"No. It's just... Sometimes Henry says the weirdest shit out of the blue, and I think we underestimated what he may or may not have remembered from... And I hate that my son was a witness to our fucked up shit. I tried so hard to protect him from that, but I guess I failed, and I worry about how it may impact him in the future. I'm such a terrible parent," she says with a sob, and I grab her arm to guide her to sit on the kid's bed.

I only know bits and pieces of the shit with Sheriff Wallace, and I have no idea what to say to that.

"Shit, I'm sorry. Really, it's the hormones. I don't know why I'm telling you this. That was the worst trauma dump ever," Jenny sniffles.

I rub my neck and tilt my head to Tommy once again. He's way better at talking about feelings than me. But to my dismay, he just makes a circular motion with his palm, mouths "talk", and backs out of the room. Some friend he is.

Jenny sniffles loudly, so I sit on the opposite side of the bed, with my back turned slightly toward her. If I'm to talk about this shit, I can't have anyone looking at me.

"You know, I've seen a lot of fucked up shit as a kid from the time I was too young to even understand how fucked up they were. My mom..." I cringe and breathe a sigh. "Her world revolved around the men she was seeing. Her whole personality could change on a whim based on the fucker she was dating at the time. He was a family man? Boom, look, here's my son. Look how adorable he is, and praise me for being such a good mother. A new guy is a party animal? Boom, let's invite all our friends and snort coke out of each other's butt cracks. Oh, this one doesn't like kids? Let's drop him off at my sister's house until the loser I'm currently fucking is done with me."

Jenny doesn't say anything, and I don't dare look at her, but somehow, I know I have her full attention.

"My point in saying this, I guess, is that she never even stopped to think how it makes me feel. I was just an afterthought. Still am. Yet, all I ever wanted from her was to acknowledge me and my needs. See me as a person and show that she worries about her son. I would honestly forgive that she subjected me to all that. I would forgive all her mistakes because she's my mom, you know? But she just doesn't care even until this day." I frown at my clasped hands and recall the last time my mother came to visit me in prison. "So when you say that you're a terrible parent... It's just ridiculous, really. Because I know what a bad mother looks like. I may not know you, but I can sense you genuinely care. You want to protect your kid. You want him to be happy. You obviously spend time with him and cater to his needs. That doesn't sound like a bad mother at all, does it? And that you're even questioning yourself on this confirms it because I can assure you those thoughts won't ever cross my mom's mind."

I chance a glance at Jenny, feeling stupid as shit for exposing myself like this, but I am glad to see there are no more ongoing tears on her face. Guess that was the goal, even if I just made an ass of myself. Lord knows that I'm not suited to guide anyone on anything. But then she surprises me by squeezing my forearm.

"Thank you for saying that. I guess it's good to see things from a perspective sometimes," she says with a small smile and retreats her hand to wipe at her face. "You're actually... There's more to you than I originally thought. Not just a brainless thug."

"Thanks?" I laugh awkwardly and stand up, ready to flee.

"The thing with Claire," she says, stopping me in my tracks. "How bad was it?"

I rub at my heart as I always do when thinking about it and look to the side. "Pretty bad," I admit.

She hums in her throat. "Did you love her?"

My heart stops for a second before it resumes its beating in high speed.

"Uh, I... Yeah," I choke out, feeling so uncomfortable. Suddenly, I feel like there's no oxygen in the room.

Again, all I get is a hum before Jenny stands up. "She sure must've loved you."

My eyes snap to her, and I feel almost dizzy. "How do you know that? Did she say anything to you? Is she-?"

"Hey!" Jenny laughs at my nervous reaction, and then her expression sobers. "I just know my best friend—all of her. The pained look in your eyes whenever the subject arrives is something that you both have in common. And I know only one feeling in this world that causes this type of hurt."

"Why... ?" I croak and then clear my dry throat. " Why are you telling me this?"

She gives me a piercing look, one that creeps me the fuck out, the same unblinking one she gave me in front of her house a few days ago.

"The why is not the real question here, Aidan. The question is, what are you going to do about it?"

"Um, I don't know," I reply, utterly confused. "I was hoping to maybe talk to her. Explain my side of the story, and... Honestly, I just want to apologize for everything. I never got a chance to do that."

Jenny looks pleased by my answer, and I have no fucking idea what's in this girl's head right now.

"All right. I can help out. But if you fuck it up or hurt her..." She points a finger at me, and I have to physically keep myself in check not to flinch away in fear.

"You'll tell Brody, and he'll beat me to a pulp," I reply with a small smile that stretches into a grin when she laughs with a shake of her head.

"Nah, dude. He would have to find your body for that first, and it would be long gone by that time," she says with a smile of her own, but her is meaner, with a cold glint in her eye. Jeez.

I blink at her two times and then smirk. "Okay, I hope it won't come to that then."

"Great," she claps her hands. "Then I'll be happy to invite you to our little party we're holding Saturday. It's supposed to be a baby shower, but since I absolutely hate that kind of mushy, fluffy, pink bullshit stuff, it's going to be a barbecue in our backyard." Then she throws over her shoulder. "You're invited too, Tommy."

He steps from around the corner with a sheepish smile. His face reddens when I throw him a stink eye. I thought he went downstairs to watch over the kid or something, but the fucking gossip stayed here this whole time.

"Thanks, Jenny," he mutters, stepping from foot to foot.

I concentrate back on the woman and address the two biggest issues with her invite. "Thanks, but I don't think your man is going to be happy with us being there. And I don't think Claire will appreciate my presence as well."

"Let me worry about the Hulk," she waves her hand in dismiss and then hesitates. "With Claire... Well, I don't think that keeping her in the safe bubble constantly is working anymore. If she doesn't face her demons, she won't ever recover and get back on her feet. I speak from experience."

Demons? I have no idea what exactly Jenny is referring to, and I want to ask her for more but don't get to because she already turned away.

"Okay, I took enough of your time already. Do what you have to do, boys. I gotta get back to Henry. See you Saturday at five. Don't be late."

Before I even open my mouth, she's gone.

We measure the kid's room and the bathroom before I make a quick sketch, and then we get the hell out of there. My head is a mess, and I feel the pressure building behind my eyelids with an ongoing headache. I try to process everything, but it's too much.

Tommy starts the car, and as soon as we're on the uneven road leading toward the city, he asks, "So, are we going to this thing?"

"It didn't sound like we have much of a choice, right? We're going."

"What are you going to say to her?" I know exactly what her he's referring to, and I close my eyes when the pain in my head sharpens.

"Fuck if I know, man," I sigh.

"I guess you better think of something good then," he states.

"Tommy?"

"Yeah?" He tilts his head in question.

"Shut the fuck up, man," I snap at him and he smiles.

The rest of the drive, the car remains silent, which is the opposite of what's happening in my head. God, I hope I can come up with a good speech and not make an idiot out of myself. Because somehow I know that Jenny gave me a chance to fix things, just as Brody gave me one when he hired me. And I know I better use it wisely because I won't be getting this opportunity again. And that fact terrifies me.

CHAPTER XVII

CLAIRE

I started riding a bicycle lately, and I'm amazed by how much did I miss out on by not ever learning to do that before.

My therapist advised me to try it out, and honestly, I'm hooked. The fact that I'm no longer dependent on Jenny or Brody to drive me everywhere is a huge plus, but that's not why I came to love it so much.

The wind in my hair, the sights passing me by, my wildly beating heart, and the healthy production of endorphins from the exercise makes me feel free and honestly happy. It kind of feels like flying.

I park my cute turquoise city bike in the garage and collect all my stuff from the little basket. I notice that Brody's car is still not here and frown. Jenny hasn't been saying anything about it, but I know she doesn't like how much he works lately. I hope he'll take it slow once the new baby comes.

Walking through the mudroom, I kick off my sandals and then enter the silent house.

"Jenny?" I call out before a sound of shushing comes from the little bathroom by the staircase. My friend emerges from it with a laundry basket and points toward the makeshift bed I sleep on.

I glance at the mess I left there and then grin when I see Henry curled up in a blanket, sleeping soundly with his toys by his little feet.

She places the basket on the floor and nods toward the kitchen. I tiptoe toward her and lift the bag.

"I brought us some dinner," I whisper. "Figured you're being too tired to cook and didn't know if the Big Guy is in yet."

She greedily grabs it from my hands and eyes the food. "Thank fucking God. You're a godsend, babe." She grabs two plates and starts filling hers with the takeout quickly. "Brody called that he'll be late. And I'm fucking starving."

I sit opposite her at the table and watch with a little smile as she devours the food. The Jenny I knew, honestly, couldn't care less about food. But pregnant Jenny? She's a beast.

"So, why is Brody staying late again? Do they have issues with the company?" It's not what I really want to ask, but I'm also scared to address the elephant in the room, which is me, obviously. I'm the elephant.

Jenny rolls her eyes. "Self-created issues, maybe. He took on too many projects because it would be a hit to his giant ego to say that they couldn't do something or needed more time to finish a house. And don't even let me start on the house rebuilding idea..."

I jab a piece of potato on my plate with a fork and then chew it slowly, eyeing the surrounding space.

"You're not a fan of the idea?"

She sighs and glares at the piece of meat she stabbed with a knife. "That's not it. I just don't agree that it has to be done as soon as possible. We could take it slow, you know? The kids could be in one room for a while. I don't think that it would be a big deal to wait a year or two. But you know Damon, he's so fucking stubborn and... proud. Thinks he needs to give us the best, or otherwise the world will surely accuse him of being a bad father or some other ridiculous bullshit."

"Yeah..." I tilt my head to the side and decide maybe it's time to address it after all. I feel strong enough to take it. "But do you think that, maybe, it has to do more with me being here?"

Jenny's head snaps up, and she looks at me with alarm. "What makes you say that?"

"Well, for one, I heard you fight a few times. Those walls aren't exactly thin, but the sound still carries sometimes. And uh... I know I'm a huge pain in the ass," I wince and rub at the scar on my right wrist, which is a habit I picked up along the way to help me whenever I'm feeling agitated. Like I need to remind myself that not every little inconvenience in life deserves to be rewarded by the want of escape; it's weird.

"Claire, I'm sorry. Brody can be a real asshole sometimes. But it's not really about you or the fact that you're staying with us. We told you that you can stay here for as long as you need to. I meant it, and he did, too. He's just worried that it's too much for me and that I'm going to snap or something."

"Would you tell me if I was?" I ask timidly, and she gives me a confused look. "Would you tell me I was becoming too much for you to handle?"

She looks at me like the thought is outlandish and shakes her head vehemently, making her curls swing from side to side. "You're never too much, Claire. I don't want you to ever think that. If anything, the fact that you came back into my life helped me heal. There was a big part of me that was still missing. And you were that fucking missing piece. You're my only family besides Damon and Henry and a big part of me. There's no scenario in which I would ever consider you too much. I hope that there will come a day when these kinds of thoughts won't even cross your mind."

My eyes fill with tears, and I bite my lip to keep myself from sobbing. "I just don't want you to have more problems because of me. Or spoil things between you two."

Jenny grabs my hand from across the table and glances to where Henry is still soundly sleeping in the living room area before giving me a look and rolling her eyes.

"Don't take this the wrong way, but there were always issues. Shitload of them, actually, and it was long before you showed up. Stop putting blame on yourself in places where it isn't needed. If my psychotic father, with a literal bomb strapped to his body, was unable to defeat us or tear us apart, nothing probably would. Couples fight, Claire, and God knows we both have a short fuse. I can assure you that those arguments would be here even if you weren't. We're fine."

When I still look doubtful, she leans in with a wicked smile on her face. "And the makeup sex after each fight is fucking amazing."

A loud snort escapes me, and she winks before she continues to stuff her face with the food.

"I guess I forgot how crazy your love story is," I say dreamily. "It's like in those movies that we used to watch. You, a beautiful yet troubled heroine. Him a broody, handsome hero ready to protect you at all costs. He swoops in to save you. Oh, God, it's so amazing."

Jenny giggles into her plate. "Babe, really, you crack me up. You watched far too many Hallmark movies. Our situation wasn't exactly dreamy. But yeah, I guess it's kind of romantic."

"So romantic," I sigh and rest my chin on my hand, dinner forgotten.

"Speaking of crazy love stories. Aidan was here," Jenny says casually and then watches for my reaction.

If she thinks I'm going to freak out or break down crying, then I'll have to disappoint her. That man is a stranger. Can't say I ever really knew him.

Lies. A voice in my mind whispers, and I tell it to shut up.

Deciding to play it cool, I clear my throat and throw, "Oh, yeah?"

She gives me a slow nod. "Yup. We chatted for a bit."

I flatten my lips to keep myself from assaulting Jenny with the onslaught of questions that would normally escape. My curious nature is constantly trying to break through, and my therapist said that being too talkative can be a sign of my mania peeking through, so I try to keep that in check lately.

What did you talk about? Did he mention me? Is he alright? Did he tell you about what he did? Is he going to be around for longer?

The way my lips tremble probably gives me away, so I decided to let just one of them to slip out and then immediately want to take it back. "Did he mention me?"

I put both of my palms on my mouth to keep it shut and blink rapidly.

Jenny smiles with satisfaction as I played straight into her hands. "He did, actually."

What did he say? What did you tell him? Did he... Oh, shut up brain!

"You know, I actually thought Brody was fucking nuts for helping him with getting him out on parole and giving him a job. But I can see why he did it now."

Brody helped him with parole? Why did he do it? Do you think Aidan is a good person, then? How were you able to forgive him?

My nostrils flare, but I still don't engage in the conversation.

"The guy seems like a good person. Maybe like all of us, he was just put in a shitty situation that he couldn't get out of, you know?" Jenny takes one last bite of her food and then adds like an afterthought. "I like him."

"I thought so too at one point, and now we're here," I say in a harsher tone than I intended.

"Yeah, you are, and I think it's about time you both deal with what happened back then," my friend says nonchalantly, unbothered by my tone.

"What's the point?" I throw impatiently.

"The point is that you are both miserable and both being held down by your past. Talk with him. Cry, yell, hit him, whatever it is that you need to do. Let him tell you his side of the story and judge it from an adult point of view. Not starry-eyed teenage Claire. You may find that some things weren't as bad as they seemed back then."

"I don't know," I look down and fidget with my hands. "I thought he was the love of my life, you know? You remember how easy it was for me to become obsessed with people as soon as they've given me the right amount of attention. And he used that against me."

"Look, that's not my place to say if the love between you was real or not. I don't know the full story. So, only you can attest to that. I'm not saying that you have to take him back. I'm just saying that you need to resolve it, or it's going to be a wound that never heals. It will fester and bring you down whenever you have a bad day or whenever someone else comes into your life."

"I'm... I'll think about it." I relent, but the thought of even being in the same room as Aidan fills me with fear. Not because of him, really. But because of me. I don't trust myself not to run into his arms just to get even a tiny snippet of how he made me feel back when I was seventeen.

"Okay. That's all I'm asking for now. To give you both a chance to move on," Jenny gets up and goes to the sink to wash her plate.

CHAPTER XVIII

"BITCH, WHAT THE FUCK?" I hiss as soon as Jenny sits down in her chair next to me.

We're sitting in the garden behind the house where my friend decided to host her baby shower slash family barbecue.

Brody's aunt and uncle arrived first to set the whole place up, bringing Jenny's friend Amelia with a bunch of kids. I was surprised to see Nora among them but also relieved when she seemed to get along with the other children, even if she lacked the ability to fool around and laugh as they played in the garden. A few of Brody's friends arrived soon after, and then Jenny's former boss Garry with his wife.

And everything was great. Until the only person that I definitely wasn't ready to face yet marched into the backyard, fitting perfectly among the rowdy group of people ready to smile at him. Then his eyes caught mine.

Aidan, who showed up with his friend Tommy, is presently sitting stiffly four places away from me, but since the table is round, he's placed practically opposite my chair.

"What?" Jenny asks innocently and digs into her cake enthusiastically without sparing me a look.

"What is he doing here?" I glance at Aidan and meet his frightened eyes before he looks away.

179

"Who, Aidan? Oh, you know... Brody and I decided to invite all his workers since they spent so much time together at the construction. They are practically a part of the family now, so..."

"Oh, yeah? I thought Brody had at least four workers, if not more. How come they aren't here?" I question and scrutinize the impassive way in which she eyes people around us from above her dessert.

"Couldn't make it," she replies easily, and I glare at her.

"You could've at least given me a heads-up."

She tilts her head to the side but still doesn't look at me directly. "Why? So you could run?"

Yes, that's exactly what I would do. But I don't voice that, not wanting to see her satisfied smirk. With a huff, I grab my plate and march toward the long table full of snacks, salads, and drinks, just to be free of my nosy best friend and Aidan's scorching looks.

I balance my plate on one hand and start filling it when I feel a presence next to me. Close. Too close.

"Hey," he says quietly, and I swear his voice awakens parts of me that stayed dormant since I was seventeen.

"Hey," I say without looking at him, and continue to layer my paper plate with food that I surely won't eat, but it gives me something to focus on.

"You look great, Claire," Aidan says and shifts his body even closer to mine.

I scoff and try to move away from him, but a hand on my arm stops me. The touch of his warm palm on my cooled skin causes me to gulp as yet another bolt snaps in my head as my body remembers the familiar touch, and memories flood my mind.

"I never thought I would see you again. After everything... But do you think that maybe we could meet sometime and... talk? I know you don't owe me anything, but..."

His voice trembles slightly in obvious nervousness, but I don't help him out; I just continue to stare at my plate.

"I tried to contact you after, you know? To explain. I guess you know that, but I just wanted to see if-"

"I didn't know that," I cut in and, for the first time, look up at him. Of course, that's a mistake.

Aidan was always very handsome, but he still had boyish features when I last saw him. Now, he's more manly. The softness that his face held is gone, and there's something new in his eyes that wasn't there before.

"You didn't know? I mean, the letters were always returned unopened. And I couldn't reach your phone or call your house. So I just assumed you didn't want to hear from me, so I stopped after some time," he rushes to say, and for a second, I have this weird need to console him. To take away all his doubts and worries.

But then I snap myself out of it.

"You assumed correctly. I didn't want to hear from you," I say slowly, and then glance at the hand that's still on my arm and lift my eyebrows at him.

"Oh," he backs away, looking as if I kicked his puppy, and again, I have to struggle with my true nature.

I'm not good at being mean, cold, or playing indifferent. I know if I stay any longer in Aidan's presence, then I will crumble and crawl into his arms. That's just who I am. A weak, spineless person who would gladly run to the person who hurt her, hoping that they won't hurt her again.

"I thought maybe if you heard my side of the story, the hurt would lessen. I never wanted to be the reason you cry, Claire. The opposite, actually. It kills me every day to think that I caused you pain. If I could somehow take it all away, I would," his eyes glaze over, and I can hear the truth in his words.

But surprisingly, even though I do believe him, it doesn't bring me any relief. No, it opens the floodgate of my anger wide open. My skin prickles with the sudden need to cause him harm.

I slap my full plate back on the table and face him fully. The mocking laugh that gets free out of my throat sounds so unnatural that I notice at least a few heads turn toward us as their conversations around the table stop. Only children continue to play around, oblivious to the shift in the atmosphere with the adults.

Aidan's mouth opens, but I beat him up to it.

"You think that this is all about you? That's rich. You think I didn't answer your stupid letters because I was sad and heartbroken? You stupid idiot. I didn't answer because I didn't fucking care. You think that you were so important to me that I would allow you to devastate me? Aidan, I'm sorry to say this, but you were only ever a distraction."

He physically recoils at my words. If I had any sense left in me, I would stop at that and go take a breather to cool down, but I'm on a roll.

"You never mattered to me. I was in a dark place when Jenny went missing, and I thought a new boyfriend could actually take my thoughts away from what's significant. I mean, it was nice while it lasted, but..." I flick my hand at him. "Don't flatter yourself by thinking that you were of such importance in my life that you actually made an everlasting impact. How long were we together, like two months? That's laughable. A stupid teenage crush, Aidan. Honestly, I feel sorry for you that after almost four years, you're still here, clearly pining over me. When, in all honesty, I forgot all about you."

My heart squeezes painfully when I say the words that I always wanted to be actually true. I didn't want to care. I didn't want to still love him. But I did. I do. And it infuriates me. Because it's not fair that I still have to go through it. That still pains me so much. Not what he did and that he lied. But that he caused us to be pulled apart.

"And what are you actually doing here, huh? Shouldn't you still be in prison, which is the rightful place that you should be at? It sickens me to see the people that you hurt giving you a chance that you obviously don't deserve."

I wish the words coming out of my mouth were true, but in reality, with each hurtful lie that comes flying out of me, I feel like my soul is bending out of shape.

Each attacking word that I spewed at Aidan caused him to move back as his face morphed from shocked to angry and then sad. After my last line, his posture changed drastically as he straightened and, with his face blank, turned away without a word.

I blink back the oncoming tears and eye the shocked faces around me, feeling like utter shit. I catch Jenny shaking her head at me in disappointment before she wobbles after Aidan. Tommy steps away from the table, too, and looks at me angrily before marching toward them.

I see the other guests exchange looks before they all try to pretend nothing happened and go back to their conversations from before. I'm thoroughly ignored as I walk away to the other side of the expanse garden and sit down on a tree log with my back to everyone.

I don't want people to see me now, so I grimace when footsteps sound behind me.

"Please leave me alone, Jenny," I throw tearfully without looking back.

"I'm too ugly to be Jenny," Brody responds before he steps in front of me. To my surprise, he doesn't look angry or disgusted with me. He should because what I said was horrible.

"I'm sorry that I disrupted your party," I mutter, ignoring the tears that annoyingly won't stop coming.

Brody doesn't say anything for a long moment before he takes a seat next to me. I expect him to reprimand me or tell me that I am no longer welcome here because my outburst was the last straw. But he doesn't speak, just looks ahead at the slowly swaying trees.

In the next minutes, I find myself staring at the treetops, too, as my breathing evens out and the new tears dry out.

"Why did you hire him?" I break the silence. It's not exactly what I want to know, but Brody seems to understand what I need to hear nonetheless. How did he find the strength to forgive the people who wronged him?

"There's no worse feeling in this world than having good intentions and trying to do what's right and still ending up being the bad guy," he replies, and I frown at him. "Good people end up doing bad things because they often find themselves in a difficult situation that they don't see a way out of. Wouldn't you agree?"

He gives me a meaningful look, and I blink.

"David Wallace was a bad man—a source of badness in more lives than I could ever count. And for a long time, I felt guilty for allowing things to go so bad. If I had caught him sooner, none of this would have happened."

"But you don't blame yourself anymore?" I prompt him when he stops talking and seems to get lost in thought.

Brody's head shakes, and he smiles. "Had to let it go. I realized he's been still tainting my life, even from the grave. And I had to admit that, just as people that came before and after me, I've been pulled into the fucked up web of his schemes. Hard to get out of once you're in. And I was an FBI agent with a military background. People like Jen, her mom, and frankly Aidan didn't stand a chance."

I bite my lip and glance at my lap, feeling like shit.

"Not that I defend what Aidan's done. I still have a scar at the back of my head to attest to just how much he fucked up. What he did was wrong; there's no question about it. And I can only assume what happened between you two back in the day. But the thing that really impressed me was that he never tried to get off the hook. And he could. Easily. But he admitted to his crimes, took the blame for the things he had done, and lost three years of his youth while thinking that he wouldn't be out until he was at least forty."

I never knew that, so I hang onto each word like a lifeline.

"I went to each sentencing. I heard statements from each member of the *Culebras* gang. None of them took responsibility, even in the face of strong evidence. And here's this artistic kid who never had parents or any other role model apart from his no-good brother, taking the blame and apologizing to me while looking straight into my eyes. I can't forget the look on his face when he heard the judge's sentencing. It was heartbreaking, not because he felt bad, but because he accepted his fate and already had given up."

"So you decided to help him?" I whisper.

Brody glances behind his shoulder, and I follow his line of sight to where his son Henry sits with the other children. I know he's not really the biological father of the kid, but you would never know that with the way he's interacting with him.

Then he looks back at me and says, "I just gave him a chance. And I have a feeling I won't regret doing that. The question is, will you do the same?"

He stands up with the help of his cane and goes back to his guests and Jenny when she starts to unwrap the received gifts for the baby. She catches my eye mid-laugh when she lifts a little pink dress and waves me over with a soft expression on her face.

I join the party and notice that no one eyes me any differently, even after my outburst. Those people accepted me as a new member of their makeshift family.

They have given me a chance.

Maybe now it's time I do the same for Aidan—one chance. And maybe I will be able to finally stop running.

CHAPTER XIX

There's a knock on my door, but I don't react, my eyes glued to the half-finished project of Brody and Jenny's bedroom. When another knock follows soon after, I begrudgingly lift my head, just now realizing that Tommy left the apartment about an hour ago, so he's not here to open it.

After I got my assigned temporary shelter place from Sandra, it wasn't long until I started to search for a better place to live. The low rent was definitely a plus in there, but that wasn't enough to wash over the fact that it was a stinky dump filled with ex-cons. The people were either trying to get out of there and turn their life back around as soon as possible, or doing shit that would surely get them back inside within weeks.

So, I was happy to get out of it when Tommy announced he was looking for a roommate. The apartment we rented is small, and it's placed in one of the shadier parts of Madison, but both of us are struggling with cash, so as long as it has a working bathroom, a place to store food, and a bed, we're all set.

On my way to the door, I glance at the calendar hanging on the fridge and have to stifle a groan. Today is the parole check-up day. Which means it's probably Sandra at the door.

I actually like the woman, and I know as far as parole officers go, it could've been much worse for me. Some social workers can be real assholes, trying to sabotage you at each step. But Sandra is... well, she's definitely not an asshole. But I do have to trudge carefully around her. The thing is, I'm not interested in what she wants from me, but I don't want to downright shoot her down in case she takes it the wrong way and becomes vindictive.

A middle-aged horny woman with issues, in my case, can mean spending the next two decades back in jail.

I check the apartment with a critical eye, noticing how untidy it is but obviously not seeing anything that could be considered incriminating in site, and open the door after the third knock comes.

"Hey, sorry about the wait... Claire?" I stare at the woman who's been occupying my mind ever since the barbecue at Brody's last week. Her harsh words still bouncing around my mind, cutting deeper and deeper each time I recall our conversation.

She honestly looks great, and for the life of me, I can't stop my eyes from checking her out. Dressed in a simple floral dress that highlights her soft feminine shape in all the right places, her hair is swept to the side, with the curled ends falling to her shoulder.

Claire smiles at me for the first time since we were teenagers, and I have to stop my hand from going to my chest when my heart squeezes painfully in longing.

There's no sight of the cruel woman from the last time, and my stupid heart instantly picks up speed as my hopes rise again.

She also looks more healthy; the color is back in her cheeks, and her eyes have that little mischievous twinkle in them that I even forgot I missed for all these years.

"Do you want to stare at me some more? Or would you prefer to let me in?"

I blink at her, confused, before jumping to action.

"Please, come in. I..." I shake my head and move to the side, allowing her to move past me.

"Nice place," she says, eyeing the living room. Her tone isn't sarcastic, but I still feel my face getting red.

I rush to get my dirty clothes off the couch so she has a place to sit and then start collecting trash in a haze as I babble nervously.

"Sorry about the mess. I didn't expect any guests to come over. Not that I am not happy to see you here. I am. Very... Happy, I mean. To see you? I don't want you to think that we're living here like pigs or something. Normally, I clean regularly, but I've been so busy with the project for Jenny and Brody that I..."

Claire giggles and takes a seat. "Aidan, it's fine. I'm sure you saw the war zone effect I had on Jenny's house. I wish I could say it's Henry making all that mess, but..." She shrugs and then looks at me expectantly.

"Um. Okay, then. Let me just put those away and..." I lift my hands full of jumbled clothes and empty candy wrappers and then turn on my heel, cursing myself in my mind all the way to my room.

Why so fucking awkward, dude? Get it together. She's here, and she's not cursing me out for everything I've done anymore, so this is a good sign, right? This can be it. Don't fuck it up.

I enter my bedroom, which doesn't look any better than the living room, and wince. The walls are full of my drawings, half of them a strange mosaic of Claire's features, with the other half presenting a frozen frame of memory also starring Claire. I would die of embarrassment if she ever saw it, so I quickly drop the clothes on the bed, not caring about the plastic wrappers entangled in them, and turn to get out and close the door before she has a chance to see into the room and realize just how obsessed I've been with her over the years.

But of course, I should know better than to trust that her curiosity and impatience won't make her go after me.

"Is this your room?" I hear before her head appears in the doorway.

I try to block her view with my body. "Yeah. Sorry, but it's really messy in here. If we could just go back to the living-"

I hear her sharp intake of breath before she asks. "Is that me?"

Hanging my head in defeat, I move to the side when she gently pushes me and walks to the wall to inspect the creepy makeshift shrine that Tommy never fails to bring up and tease me about whenever we end up talking about my failed relationship with Claire.

"Um, it's not what you think," I say lamely and rub at my face.

"I think... it's beautiful, Aidan," she says softly after a pause. "When did you make all this? I don't remember you making these when we were together."

I take a deep breath to steady myself and face her. "They're from my time in prison. I've got lots of spare time, so..."

Her hand lifts to trail a finger down the curvy line of her upper lip in one of the drawings. "I always loved your art, Aidan. But this is incredible. I can see you've gotten even better with time."

"As I've said. Lots of time to practice. And lots of time to regret the things that I did wrong. Also, plenty of time to fantasize about how things could have been if I wasn't a complete spineless, cowardly moron." I can't stop the last words from landing from my mouth, and they make Claire turn around to look at me sharply.

"Isn't it the worst feeling in the world to be the villain of your own story?" She asks wistfully.

"You have no idea," I reply, feeling slightly defeated.

"I just might," she smiles at me sadly. With one last look at my drawings, she leaves my room.

I step into the living room after her, apprehension causing me to hesitate. The mood has visibly shifted now, and I can tell that whatever she came here for, she's ready to get down to it. And it scares me beyond reason.

"So, uh, how did you know where I live?" I ask when she doesn't immediately start talking.

"I asked Brody," she answers simply and eyes me with a serious expression.

I try not to fidget under her scrutiny and stand ramrod straight as if I were in front of a judge, not daring to even breathe.

A small smile painted on her face. "You look like you're waiting for a sentence," she jokes, clearly reading my mind.

"Aren't I, though? In a way?"

Claire hums in her throat. "So, I've been thinking a lot lately about the past and everything that happened. But I was also thinking about the future, which is kind of new for me. I stopped considering having one years ago."

She laughs in a self-deprecating way, and I frown. I have no idea where this is going.

"There are things... Bad things that I didn't share with you either, Aidan. I've been so angry with you. Not even because of what you did. But because you never felt it was safe to tell me about it. And that angered me to no end. Which was hypocritical of me..."

I tilt my head to the side. "I don't understand."

Claire looks down at her knees before she taps the space next to her, indicating for me to sit. Slowly, I take the place next to her, as if I was approaching a frightened animal.

She surprised me by grabbing my hand right away and looking me in the eye. The deep sadness in her eyes chills me to the bone, and without hesitation, I squeeze her small palm in mine to show my support for whatever she's struggling with, even though I may be the last person worthy of consoling her.

"I was a hypocrite because I was angry at you for lying to me or omitting the truth, when I was doing the exact same thing."

"What do you mean?"

She licks her lips and visibly shudders before going for it. "Aidan, I'm bipolar. I knew it long before we were a couple. And I struggled with my mental health even back in Alaska as a child. I struggled all throughout our relationship, even taking it out on you a few times. And I'm sorry I didn't tell you. It wasn't fair."

Bipolar? I've heard of it, but I don't exactly understand what that means for Claire in particular.

"Can you... ? Uh, explain what that means?"

Claire sits straighter and uses her free hand to point at her forehead. "It just means that my brain consists of two constantly polarizing parts. It's either super happy to downright manic, or it's in deep depression. My brain can't balance the chemical processes on its own, so it's either this or that. My mom..." she looks away and exhales heavily. "My mom had it. And she didn't treat it. At least not since I remember. She committed suicide when I was thirteen."

I take a deep breath before exhaling in a whoosh. "Jesus, Claire. I'm so sorry, baby. I didn't know-"

"That's not all," she cuts me off, and her eyes come back to me with a new look. Fear. "Ever since that happened, it was actually hard for me to feel bad about it. To feel grief or sadness because she left. And it was because... I was jealous."

My head moves back in shock. "Jealous?"

Claire nods her head, looking uncertain. "I know it will sound wrong. It is wrong. But I was jealous that she was brave enough to do this. To leave this world behind and be free."

"Claire, you can't mean..." my throat squeezes painfully, making me choke on my words. The thought of the most incredible woman that I know, the woman that I love, having those thoughts is absolutely inconceivable.

"I did it too," she adds then quietly and shivers. "After your arrest... I cut my wrist-"

"No!" I drop her hand and jump to my feet. I point an accusatory finger in her way. "Don't you fucking say it, Claire!"

I feel something heavy press on my chest, and I stumble as far away as I can from her. It feels like there's no air in the room like all oxygen has been removed with Claire's confession.

I can't believe it. I did this. I pushed her over the edge. So focused on keeping her that I was ready to overlook her pain. Her struggles. I was so eager to justify it with some teenage anxiety and stupid shit. While my girl was in pain. And then she...

"Hey, Aidan!" I open my eyes to find Claire's face right in front of me. "That's not true. Okay? You didn't let me finish. I'm fine. I'm here, aren't I?"

I realize I must've expressed some of my internal turmoil out loud. Claire's hand connects with my cheek as she wipes a tear that escapes my eye before she sighs.

"You're not responsible for what I did, Aidan. I did blame you in the past because it was easier that way. The truth is I would've probably done it even if I didn't meet you or even if we stayed together and things were fine. It would've been one silly fight, and I would snap. Things were bad even before Jenny disappeared. The thing that I had to understand myself was that I was the only person who had the power to get me out of this. That this is my fight. Sure, it's easier to go round after round in the ring if you have people cheering you on from the corner. But essentially, it is me who is standing in the way of getting well. I need to be strong to continue the battle. And back then, I just wasn't. I saw the easy way out, and I took it."

She rolls the right sleeve of her dress and presents me with a straight, slightly jagged white scar going from the top of her wrist to almost half the length of her forearm.

For the first time, shame enters her delicate face, and I take her wrist in mine to kiss the spot gently. "I'm so sorry, Claire. For everything. I wish things were different."

"Me too," she replies solemnly before grabbing onto my hand and pulling me back to sit on the couch.

Reluctantly, I let her but turned my head away to wipe my tears, conscious of the fact that she already saw them but wanting to appear stronger in case she needed me to lean on.

I hear her slow breaths as she waits patiently for me to get myself together. It isn't an easy task. I'm still shaken to my core, but I'm also aware that it had to be even harder for Claire to say out loud. So if she can face the day, so will I. There will be time to process it later.

"So, what happens now?" I ask in a lighter tone.

A strange look crosses her face before it goes blank. "I want you to take me somewhere."

"Whe-?" A knock on the door stops me from questioning her.

"Are you expecting more company?" Claire asks and stands up.

"No," I shake my head and go to answer the door, aware that Claire is hot on my heels. I smirk to myself because this curiosity thing is such a Claire thing.

But then my lips downturn when I open the door and see Sandra standing there, looking like a freshly divorced cougar ready to get her revenge on her unfaithful husband as she goes out clubbing. With Claire's presence, I completely forgot about the visit.

"Hi, Aidan," she coos, and without waiting for an invitation, walks past me, her boobs rubbing on my arm purposefully in the process.

I close the door after her and eye her, unable to hide my displeasure with the fact that of all the times she's checking on me, she had to choose today to look like an escort.

I throw an apologetic look toward Claire, but it goes unnoticed as she's busy eyeing the woman coldly before she crosses her arms.

"Claire, this is my parole officer, Sandra," I'm quick to inform as the two women have some weird nonverbal conversation with each other.

"Is that so?" Claire asks with her eyebrow raising to dangerous levels.

"Hi, I'm Sandra," the older woman extends her hand for Claire to shake with a friendly smile in place.

After a pregnant pause, when I already started to think this would turn even more awkward, Claire uncrosses her arms and quickly shakes the woman's hand.

"Nice to meet you," she says in a tone that indicates that it's anything but nice indeed, and Sandra chuckles before focusing on me.

"You didn't forget about me, did you?" Sandra asks, and I want to groan at her choice of words.

"No, Sandra. I didn't forget about being on parole. And yes, I was expecting your visit. I just didn't know you'd show up so late and..." I wave at her dress, thinking her outfit speaks for itself.

The woman whirls around and says, "You like?"

I want to shake the woman, but all I do is glare at her before mouthing sorry to Claire, who, now to my surprise, looks close to amused.

"So, anyway. Who's your friend? I didn't know you were seeing anyone?" Sandra questions over her shoulder as she walks to the living room. "You know I also need to keep watch on whom you're associating with, right?"

"Claire is... an old friend of mine," I reply, getting annoyed with Sandra as she starts snooping around the place.

"Really?" She lifts her head from one of the drawers she's rummaging through. "So you know each other from school or...?"

"Yup." I say, just as Claire says, "Not exactly."

We share a look, and I try to convey the message to Claire not to say anything because I know Sandra is like a dog with a bone. She's not going to let it go.

"Actually, we used to be together before Aidan went to prison," Claire says with a shrug, and Sandra snaps to attention, forgetting about pretending to search the place.

"Oh, that sounds like an incredible story. Young love, full of passion, ripped apart by the circumstances," Sandra says excitedly and struts over to Claire on her high heels. "Tell me, does the passion between you two last the test of time? Was it even better than before when you first rejoined?"

I almost choke on my saliva at that and start coughing. What the fuck is wrong with this woman?

"Don't know yet. I guess we'll have to see," Claire responds without missing a bit.

Wait? What? Does she mean what I think she means, or is she only saying that to mess with Sandra?

"Oh. I get it. You'll have to tell me how it went then. With details. I looove love."

"Sure thing," Claire chirps.

"If, for some reason, you can't get the fire going anymore, don't hesitate to call for me. Aidan has my number. For me, three isn't a crowd; it's a magic number. Anyway, I won't disturb your time any longer. It's a Friday night, and I'm dressed to impress, so I'll see you both around," Sandra smiles happily and then stops before leaving. "Oh, Aidan. Be sure to stop by my office next week. I have some paperwork for you to fill out. Okay, byeee."

"Bye, Sandra," Claire calls with a wave.

The door closes, and I whip my head toward Claire.

"What the fuck?"

"I really like your parole officer. She's cool," she says, genuinely seeming to think so, and I eye her like she's grown a second head.

"Claire, I'm pretty sure she just invited us to have a threesome. With her. A threesome."

"Yes, I think she did," Claire shrugs. "So, are you ready to go?"

"Go?" I ask, stupefied.

"Yes. I want you to take me somewhere. Remember?" She asks softly.

"Oh. Um, yeah. I didn't know if... Okay, just give me a second."

CHAPTER XX

I WAS SURPRISED WHEN Claire told me to take her to the lake, where I first showed her my art. That night was burned into my entire existence, and I'm apprehensive about coming back in case things go wrong and the memory of us making love under the stars surrounded by fireflies will be tainted.

But I could never say no to Claire. So what she wants, she will get. Other than that, she willingly wanted to spend time with me, and my grandmother used to tell me never to look a gift horse in the mouth, so I decided to go with the flow.

I've been borrowing Brody's company truck and was told specifically to only use it for work. Well, I guess I better not scratch it on the thick bushes that overgrew the narrow dirt road leading toward the pier.

"So, are you in contact with Saint?" Claire asks from the passenger seat as I try to remember where is the little clearing by the forest where I can leave the car.

"There's not much that we can say to each other anymore. We wrote a few letters back and forth while I was inside, but with time, it turned out how little we had in common. Less than I originally thought, to be honest. Also, the contact with him can be difficult sometimes. Unlike the rest of us, Santiago ended up in a federal prison in California because he was already wanted in three other states for some shit he did years before he took me in. And to top that, when I last called the facility after getting out myself, I was informed that he was in solitary because of misbehaving or some shit. Supposedly, he's been doing that a lot, so there's that... Okay, here we are."

At last, I spot the little field of grass with a view of the trees and a lake and turn off the engine.

Claire doesn't wait for me; she just gets out and confidently struts toward the wooden pier. Just as I did all those years before, she tests to see if the wood is strong enough to support our weight and waves me in to join her.

It's late, so a few fireflies already made their appearance, blinking slowly in unison in the distance.

I sit down cross-legged, mirroring Claire's pose, and watch the peaceful scene playing in front of me. I take a deep breath of the fresh air and am once again struck with amazement when it comes to being outside. Free and just able to breathe.

My eyes drink in the tranquil landscape before they travel to Claire, who continues to stare ahead in wonder.

She's so beautiful that my hands itch to draw her sitting here, surrounded by the mostly untouched nature. So pure.

I must've been staring at her too hard because suddenly, her head moves toward me. Her eyebrows pulled together.

"I just wanted to see if any of this was real, you know?" She asks, barely audible, and I lean closer to hear her better.

I wish I would've taken a blanket or at least a jacket because it's getting cold, and I notice the way she shivers. Last time we were here, it was almost summer. Now, we're nearing autumn, and the wind is already carrying cold crispness with the air.

"You mean the fireflies?"

Claire shakes her head but doesn't give me an answer. She continues to watch the glowing insects with a soft expression before her eyes mist with tears, and I stiffen.

"Hey, what is it? Do you want to come back?" I'm ready to jump to my feet.

"No," she whispers, and glances at me. "They're just as beautiful as they used to be."

"So are you," I reply automatically.

I know we've been here before. It's a peculiar feeling. Like nothing has changed, and at the same time, all is different.

The smile she gives me is sad. "I'm not like the girl you used to know anymore."

"I'm not the man you used to know too, yet here we are."

"Yeah," she sighs and scoots closer to envelop my hand in hers. My mouth turns dry at the small touch, and I have to suppress a shiver of my own. "Here we are."

"Claire... There's been so much that I wanted to tell you, I..." I start, and she stops me by putting a finger on my lips.

"Don't Aidan. Just let's not talk about it here," she says softly before turning to kneel in front of me. Then my eyes widen in surprise when she leans in to put her mouth on mine in a simple, short kiss.

"Claire, what is happening?" I mutter against her lips and glance at her eyes. They are clear and full of intent, and I have to gulp.

"You made me feel loved, Aidan. Cherished. Beautiful. Desired. Right here under the sky, surrounded by those mesmerizing creatures. I want to feel that again."

I stare at her, completely speechless, unable to move a muscle. My body yearns for her. I've spent literal years dreaming about this girl. I imagined her curves, the way her body felt under me, recalling the little noises of pleasure she made whenever I touched her just the way she liked. Yet, I'm unable to make a move.

In my head, she became this ghost. A fragile spirit that will fade as soon as I blink. One wrong move, and she will be gone. And I will be left alone again to rot in despair.

She must see the indecision in my eyes because she touches her forehead to mine and whispers, "Please, Aidan. I need you."

Slowly, I lift my hand to touch her soft cheek and watch as her eyes close when she leans into my palm. Then I cover the distance between our lips and kiss her tenderly. I switch position so she can straddle me, and the kiss turns from sweet to passionate, and ends up on the verge of desperate. We both start to tear each other's clothes off, oblivious to the cold temperature, and before I can think it through, I lie Claire's delicate body on the wooden boards and enter her in one swift motion.

Her body is hot and ready for me, and we both moan loudly, the sound mixing with the noisy nature around us. She clings to me as if she's scared that I will dissolve, her eyes never leaving mine.

I feel her squeeze around me and watch her air intake increase each time I push into her. Her face is flushed, her tousled hair a mess around her arms, and I can't believe how much my memory tricked me. Not even the hottest dreams about Claire or the most vivid memories can hold a candle to the real deal.

Claire's body feels like heaven, and when her internal walls squeeze almost painfully around my dick with the violent way she orgasms, screaming loudly, I can't help but let go, too, emptying myself inside her.

I twist our bodies so that I'm not crushing her into the hard surface of the pier with my body, and Claire ends up lying next to me, with her head supported by my arm. It's far from comfortable here, but she doesn't seem to mind as she caresses my torso with her hand and gazes at the slowly appearing stars in the sky.

"Thank you," she whispers after some time. "I needed that validation. The thought of it all being in my head was driving me crazy."

"What do you mean?" I squint at her in the semi-darkness.

"The things I told you about my... illness." She tilts her head away and hesitates. "When we first met, I was very disturbed, Aidan. My mental health was deteriorating. And now, when I'm starting to see the world in a more sober way, sober also being the keyword in my case, I wondered what was really between us back then. A big part of me worried that it was all in my head. Even though my heart knew the truth."

Well, that doesn't sound too good. Because I know for a fact that everything was painfully real for me. So, I'm apprehensive to ask the next question, but I need to know.

"And what's the verdict? Was it real?" I'm sure she can hear the tremor in my voice.

"It was," she sighs and then kisses me on my peck before sitting up. "Thank you for that, Aidan. The thought of all of those beautiful moments between us being just a hoax killed me each day, you know? I feel like I've been set free. Like I can start over now."

A feeling of panic envelops me, and I sit up, too, when she stands up and starts to put on her clothes.

"But where does this leave us then? Because it sounds like you're saying goodbye, Claire."

She smiles without a word, gives me a hand to help me to my feet, and then passes me my pants. As she watches me dress, a weird expression crosses over her features, as she has already distanced herself from here, and I fucking hate it.

As soon as I'm fully dressed, she turns toward the footpath leading to where I left the car, and I follow her, dreading what will surely come next.

I turn on the ignition to heat the car but don't move the gear just yet; instead, I turn my head to glance at Claire, finding her already looking my way.

"Claire..."

"I need time," she says, extending her hand to massage the frown between my eyebrows. "This isn't a goodbye, okay? More like a new beginning. But we need to take things slow this time. Build everything from the ground up. No secrets, no psychotic shit. Just me and you."

"But what does that exactly entail?"

"I don't know," she laughs. "I've never done this before. But maybe you can start off by asking me out on a date or something? That seems like a good place to start, I would say."

"Really?" My heart starts beating loudly as a wave of hope crashes over me, making me almost leap across the seat to kiss the hell out of her. But then I remind myself of everything she just said and refrain from doing that. Instead, I pump the air happily like a complete dork, making Claire giggle.

"Yes, really. Now take me home, please."

"Your wish is my command," I state, and drive us back.

As soon as I pull the car up in Brody's driveway, the light in the living room turns on, and Jenny wobbles onto the porch, looking worried. Her hair is a mess, and the bathrobe she has on her can barely conceal her large stomach. I don't know anything about pregnancies and babies and stuff, but to me, she looks ready to burst any time now.

"You're gonna be fine?" I ask Claire before she can get out.

"I think so." Then, she glances at Jenny with a small frown. The woman watches us with a pensive look and crosses her arms. "I'm tired of being her burden, you know? She's my best friend, and I appreciate her help. But Jenny has a lot on her plate as it is. Maybe I should move out..."

The thought worries me after everything she told me. "Are you ready to do that?"

She mulls over it before lifting her shoulders. "Not really, no. But maybe it's time."

"If you're not ready, just wait it out. I don't know Jenny as well as you do, but I doubt she sees you as a burden. She clearly loves you."

"Yeah..." She smiles softly. "Anyway, thank you for taking me to the pier. Goodnight, Aidan."

"Goodnight, Claire. I'll call you tomorrow, okay?" My voice doesn't disguise how lovesick I am already, yet I don't care.

"You better," she winks and exits the car to meet with her pregnant friend.

They exchange a few words, and then Jenny nods her head with a smile before engulfing Claire in a side hug and turning them toward the door. Before they go inside, Jenny looks over her shoulder and gives me a small wave as she mouths, "Thank you."

I wave back and then reverse the car as soon as the door closes behind them. As I drive home, I feel lighter than I've felt in years. Maybe ever, actually. I even turn on the radio and sing some sappy love ballad that's playing. I'm already thinking of all the ways I could make Claire happy and all the places I can take her. My options are limited because of the short funds I possess currently, but somehow, I doubt Claire would care about going to a fancy restaurant.

My head fills with all this romantic bullshit I know Claire loved to watch in those Hallmark movies. I can't wait to pull off something like that and watch her eyes gleam in happiness. Amazing what love can do to a man.

CHAPTER XXI

It's been four weeks since Aidan and I decided to give our love another try. And so far, it's the best decision I have made in years.

Sometimes, it feels like we picked up where we left off with how comfortable and real we can act around each other. But most times, our relationship is so much better now that we've both matured and learned from our previous mistakes.

Whenever we're apart, I feel like half of me is missing, and I wish we could fast-forward to the place where we share our lives and our space again. But we agreed to take things slow, so that's what we're doing.

We haven't even had sex since the trip to the pier, and I can feel I won't be able to last much longer. Every time Aidan kisses me goodbye after another date, he leaves me there on Jenny's doorstep, panting and needy. And I know the next time that happens, I will probably just drag him to the closest isolated place.

Funny how the right man can turn me into a sex-crazed zombie. When I was in Chicago, I didn't even like the thought of being touched by a man. And now all I fantasize about is when I will again feel Aidan's body move against mine.

Today, we have another date, and Aidan claimed this one will be special, so I know it's time we move to the next level. Although, I don't know what can be considered more special than the last date we were on. He took me to an amusement park and let me go multiple times on each ride until I puked the mixture of popcorn and cotton candy into the nearest trash can. Good times.

But if he's going to up his game, then I decided to do the same and buy myself some sexy lingerie for tonight.

I started to help out a bit at the diner Jenny used to work at to make some money, and slowly transitioned from being the parasite feeding off Jenny and Brody's hospitality to being an actual responsible adult. I'm taking it slow and only working for a few hours when Garry the boss needs me.

But I made enough now to take myself on a little trip into town and splurge on something sexy for my man.

Since Jenny took the car to drive herself to the last checkup before the baby comes, I just scribbled her a quick note, grabbed my bicycle from the garage, and rode downtown.

Last time I was shopping with Jenny, I noticed a nice shop with lingerie that looked just perfect, and now I walk into the place already set on what I want.

The cute little costume looks remarkable. I can't wait to see Aidan's face when he undresses me tonight. God, I need to make a move on if I want to be ready before he arrives at Jenny's.

I pay and quickly get out of the store when a male voice freezes me on the spot. "Found you."

My head whips toward the silhouette of a man standing beside me, right where I left my bicycle.

Nico Ramirez stands there looking very well put together if it weren't for a weird metal brace around his leg. By his side stands a tall bodyguard, looking ready to tackle me, and I gulp before I start to frantically look around for a way to escape. Then I remember the lady at the store and take a step back.

"You don't want to do that, Claire," Nico warns, swiping his eyes over me. "You should come with us."

I snort and give him an incredulous look. "Why would I ever do that?"

"Because we know what you've been hiding," he states simply, and I feel the blood leaving my face. "I would hate for something to happen to your friend. How far along is she?" Nico's head tilts to the side like he's genuinely curious, and we're just friends catching up.

My mouth opens, but nothing comes out. I feel faint and nauseous. This can't be happening. Again.

Why did I think that they would just leave me be? Oh, fuck. Nora...

She's been staying with Amelia and her family for a while, since she's been getting along so well with her kids. I visited her a few times, but when I noticed that I only brought her pain and bad memories with my presence, I stopped.

How long were they watching me? Do they know where she is? Is their whole family in danger, too?

"Come on, Claire. There's no need to look like you're ready to pass out. Nothing bad will happen to your friends. I promise. But..." he makes a dramatic pause and smiles. The fucker. "You need to be a good girl and come with us. No funny business. One wrong move, and they're all dead, you got me?"

I just stare at him, breathing harshly, and he snaps. "You got me?"

My legs carry me toward Nico, and I hang my head. I can only hope that by surrendering, I will protect everyone.

I WENT WILLINGLY, SO there was no duct tape binding or stuffing me into the trunk.

Nico called his brother from the front seat that they'd got me and was silent for the entire ride back to Chicago.

Over an hour later, the car stopped in front of a nice-looking house where more security guards were already waiting by the entrance, ready to intercept me.

The fact that no one even bothered blindfolding me or talking quietly around me tells me that I won't be getting out of here. At least not outside a body bag. If there's even anything left of me when they're done.

I should cry or rage or something, but all I feel is calm as they lead me through the house and down the stairs into a cold basement. I would probably cry and range if they caught me a month ago, but nothing holds that power over me now.

Aidan's love is with me—the memories of his face, his gentle touch, and his sweet words of affection. No one will take that away from me.

Nico walks with me into the cold cell, and I smile tauntingly when I notice how hard it was for him to come down here because of the leg.

I eye the weird brace around his knee theatrically and ask, "How's the leg, Nico?"

"You think that's funny? We'll see how amused you'll be after Sergio is done with your dumb ass," he spits.

"Always in need of the big brother to deal with the tougher stuff," I sigh. "Fine, bring him in then. I would rather be threatened by a real man, anyway."

"You fucking bitch," he says and charges at me, but then one of the guards steps in to intercept the blow he wanted to throw.

The meaty guy barely flinches and calmly states, "The boss said she's not to have any visible marks on her."

"Fucking fine," Nico says, and after one last murderous look gets out with the guard in tow, locking the cell after them.

I take a deep breath and look around. Nice dungeon. I guess it's perfect for torture and keeping your enemies in until they starve.

I check the lock on the door, just to verify it's truly closed, and then sit down on the cobblestone cold floor. My teeth are already chattering even before the temperature slowly drops in the room as hours pass.

Finally, I hear footsteps before the man in charge himself walks in. I shoot to my feet, and we eye each other silently before he smirks.

"Hello, Claire. I'm so glad we were able to track you in the end."

"Sergio," I say as a way of greeting. "Why exactly am I here?"

I glance at the two guys who enter the room and stand on each side of their boss.

"I feel like we got off on the wrong foot, Claire. Don't you think? But I think that we can still work together to smooth everything out."

"Fuck you. There won't be any smoothening happening. If you want to kill me, just do it, and stop fucking talking," I snap at him and lift my chin defiantly. Man, I think Jenny is rubbing off on me because I didn't even know I could speak like that in the face of grave danger.

Sergio looks surprised by my words, too, before he barks with loud laughter. Then his face gets serious, changing so rapidly that I question whether the humor was ever there. His eyes roll over me with interest.

"You know, come to think of it, I should actually thank you."

"Thank me?" I splutter and then blanch when he reaches into his pocket. Sergio seems to take pleasure in my reaction and lifts a cigar.

One of the guards brings a lighter close to his face, and we all watch as he drags on it before puffing out a small cloud.

Sergio gazes away as if in thought and waves a hand, causing the smoke to swirl around us, making him look like an evil wizard drawing a spell for a moment.

"Yes, thank you. You see. It's easy to let your guard down when you've been on top for so long. When you're a shark, all you do is wait out for other, bigger sea creatures to circle you around. Having eyes on them, you wouldn't think to keep an eye on the smaller fishes. You wouldn't even notice their existence!" He booms, making me jump. "And you took advantage of that. And then took something of mine. Did it right under my nose. And to top it all off, you managed to escape us when we found you. Because even after the stunt you pulled at the club, we still underestimated you."

He goes quiet for a while, and I wonder where he's going with it.

"Again. Another lesson. So yes. Thank you. This time around, we won't be making the same mistakes again."

He jerks his head at me, and I flinch when a pair of strong palms grab me by the shoulders from behind, immobilizing me.

"What are you going to do?" I can't keep the shaking out of my voice, even if it kills me to show him my weakness. Ramirez hears this, of course, and smiles cruelly.

"You see, Claire, I'm a businessman foremost. I have businesses to manage, people on the payroll who depend on me, and clients who are willing to pay for what I can provide them with. The girl you took..." he clicks his tongue and walks closer before grabbing my chin and making me look at him. "I already found a buyer for her. He was not pleased when I told him what occurred at the hands of a very nosy bartender at one of our strip clubs. But we came to an arrangement that will help me save my face while serving my client with the merchandise he ordered."

My breaths turn harsh as anger spikes in me to dangerous levels. Merchandise? That's what Nora was to this man?

"You're lucky the coke didn't take away your innocent, childish features yet because my buyer actually got excited upon seeing your photograph. Personally, I don't see the appeal, but as they say in retail, the customer is always right. So, who am I to burst his bubble?"

"You're crazy if you think I'm going to just sit quiet and be bought by some disgusting motherfucker."

Sergio's mouth twitches slightly as if my outburst is laughable to him. As if I'm a joke.

"Yes. That's the problem, isn't it? You've got too much life in you. You have lots of fights hidden in that little body. A spark. It's probably what got my stupid brother so infatuated with you in the first place. But..." he lifts his finger as if to stop me from talking, even though I wasn't going to. "I promised my client you will be docile, just as the child would be. Defenseless. So we'll keep you for a while and make some... adjustments."

"Adjustments?" I parrot, and my breath hitches when he reaches into his suit jacket again.

This time, he's going to shoot me. But it's not the gun he retrieves from his pocket. It's a syringe, and I feel myself tensing.

"What's that?" I eye the thin object.

He taps it twice and holds it right in front of my face.

"Your friend told me about your struggles with party drugs. And told me a bit about your story. Pitiful, really." He glances at my right wrist, and I don't think I can imagine the burning feeling on the part of my skin that wears signs of my darkest moment. Sergio grins at my visible discomfort. "She also mentioned your aversion to anything stronger. But I'm sure it won't be long before you break your resolve."

"What did you do with Christy?" I hear myself asking.

What she did to me was terrible, but I considered her a friend before the addiction took her away, and I still feel the worry about her well-being gnawing at me.

"After your friend happily shared every single detail about your life, she wasn't needed anymore," Ramirez states.

"You let her go?" The hope in my voice is unmistakable.

"Hmm, yes." He responds, and I exhale loudly. "Such a shame what happened to her after that. I'm sure the neighbors were shocked to find her swinging from a streetlight pole by your building complex. I wonder how she got up there," he muses, rubbing his chin.

"You're a monster," I choke out and blink rapidly to get rid of the moisture gathering in my eyes.

He leans into my ear and whispers, making me shiver, "We all have a monster within us, little girl. You should know that by now. The question is: Will you unleash it on others or rather destroy yourself? I choose the former. Weak people like you will always choose the latter."

I swallow the heavy ball of grief and fury down and watch him as he moves away. My brows furrow when he bends in front of me and places the syringe at my feet.

"It will be fun to watch you struggle," he says, leaving the room.

I feel the man who was holding me this whole time release me before he follows his boss.

My knees shake, and tripping, I move to the wall that's furthest from the door before sliding down to my butt. There are so many things that circle my mind at this moment, but one peaks through above everything else. Aidan.

His happy face when I told him I was willing to try again. The way he looked at me on our first date when I started to blabber the full plot of the film, even though he was there next to me at the cinema to watch it too. The way his eyes glimmer when he thinks about something naughty. The way his body felt at the pier.

I love him so much. I want to be strong for him.

Despite my will to ignore the little syringe, my eyes move to it, and I gulp. Instantly, a little unwanted voice appears at the back of my mind. Calling for me to just pick it up and make it all better. Make the pain and fear go away.

But I won't do it. I can't.

I need to stay strong. For Aidan. For Jenny. And most importantly, for myself.

I turn my body away and lean my head on the cold wall before I allow the exhaustion to pull me under.

CHAPTER XXII

AIDAN

I swallow the nerves and straighten my tie one more time in the little mirror before I exit the car I parked in front of my boss's house. The suit I bought especially for this occasion isn't exactly uncomfortable, but it does feel strange. I don't remember ever wearing something so pricey.

I grab the small bouquet of pink roses from the back seat and step on the doorstep to knock.

Claire always says she doesn't need fancy. That all she wants is to spend time together, and I believe her, but I still want to give her the princess treatment I know she deserves. Even if it's just this once. So, for tonight, I got us a reservation at a restaurant that is normally way out of my price range.

I've been doing some extra work on the side without telling anyone besides Tommy. Partially because I need the money but also because it keeps me occupied enough not to want to run back to Claire as soon as we're apart. She wants to take things slow, and I respect her wishes.

My girl loves surprises, so the only thing I told her was to wear a dress. I bounce lightly on my feet to shake off the excitement at seeing her face as I wait for the door to open.

However, it's not Claire opening the door, but Jenny looking spooked.

"I was just about to call you," she says and swallows.

"Call me? Why? What happened?" I look behind her shoulder, searching for Claire. "Is Claire not ready yet?"

"She's not here," Jenny says, and my eyes move back to her slowly. Now that I give her a closer look, I notice that she's not just spooked. She's actually shaken to the core.

"Where is she? What happened?" I step inside and look around as if Claire were hiding around somewhere.

Jenny closes the door and goes to sit down on the couch. Her hands go to her ginormous belly, and she moves them up and down in a soothing gesture.

"I don't know. She wasn't here when I came back from the doctor's. There was a note left on the kitchen counter stating that she was going to pick something up from a store. At first, I wasn't really worried. You know Claire likes her cycling trips to the city, but it has been hours. And I know she was excited about your date." Jenny's voice sounds almost monotonous, drastically at odds with her terrified face.

My heartbeat speeds up as all the dark scenarios run through my head, every possible accident and occurrence making an appearance.

"Have you tried calling her?" I ask, and I am already taking out my phone out of my pocket.

Jenny nods and bites her lip. "I have a feeling something bad happened."

The calm way she said it pissed me off, and I snap at her, "Don't say shit like that." Then I click on Claire's number, and when the automatic voice picks up immediately, I hang up and try again, but to the same effect.

"Where's Brody?" I ask while I shoot Claire a text message asking her to call me back.

"He took the car to look for her. About an hour ago," is her quiet response. Her hands massage her belly faster, and her breath speeds up as a sheen of sweat appears on her forehead.

"Hey, Jen, are you-?" Jenny's ringtone interrupts me, and with surprising agility for her size, she springs from the couch to walk into the kitchen and answer it.

"Have you found her?" She says to the receiver, and a painful ball of fear grows in my stomach at the face she makes after hearing whatever was said on the other end.

She glances at me swiftly and, in a breathy voice, says, "Yeah, Aidan's here. We're going now. No, it's okay. Give us five minutes."

Jenny ends the call and goes to grab the keys, and motions to the door. "Come on, Brody found something. You need to drive us because I can't reach the wheel with the stomach."

"Wait, what did he find?" I go after her and wait for her to answer as I open the passenger door to the company truck that's practically become mine now and help her get in.

"Claire's bicycle. But there's no sight of her. Come on, we gotta move," she says, squeezing her belly again.

I try to stay calm and not crash the car as I follow Jenny's mumbled directions, but it's getting harder and harder to keep the rising panic at bay.

When we park outside a small building with a few stores and a small market to the side, I notice Claire's bicycle leaning by Brody's car as the man himself talks to a small Asian woman. He nods his head as she points to somewhere and then shakes her hand.

The woman walks away before we get to him, and my first words are, "Does she know what happened to Claire?"

"That woman owns the apartment above the store. She happened to see a small blonde girl getting inside an SUV with two men," he informs me, clearly in his police mode. His eyes search my face before he looks at Jenny and frowns. "Sweetheart, are you okay?"

"The fuck is she talking about," I growl before Jenny can answer him. "What SUV?"

"I'm fine," Jenny waves a hand when Brody opens his mouth, probably to tell me to watch my tone. "But, exactly what Aidan said. What fucking SUV?"

"I only know that it was black," he replies. "Oh, and that one of the guys had a metal brace."

"A brace? Something like a cast?" Jenny inquires, her shoulders hunching slightly.

"Yeah, on his leg. It was quite big, and the woman thought it looked odd because the man was wearing a fucking suit underneath it."

"Oh, fuck. It's them. They fucking found her." She covers her mouth, and her eyes fill with tears.

"Who is them? And what do you mean by 'found her'?" I ask her and Brody, but the man seems just as confused as I am.

Jenny glances around in fright and then says quietly, "There's more to the Nora story... But here is not a good place to discuss this."

IT'S BEEN THREE DAYS since we came to Chicago, and Brody set up an impromptu office in the motel room adjoining mine. He easily slipped back into the FBI agent mode and switched between making phone calls to clicking away on his laptop to scribbling something on a pad before putting it on the pile of documents and print-outs.

All I could do, however, is prove how useless and powerless I am in a situation like that. I've been pacing around the room, waiting for Brody to find where they are holding Claire. The only thing I could do was run errands like arranging food and taking phone calls when Brody was too busy.

When we arrived in the city, I was set on going to the police straight up, but Brody was quick to shoot down that idea. He's certain that men, like the ones who took Claire, are surely having someone on their payroll within the police department. Otherwise, they wouldn't be able to climb as high.

Reluctantly, I agreed to his plan to start from a legal angle, which basically means that Brody tries to find out what he can by simple research—calling people who might know something and asking around the place where Claire used to live before we resolve to the use of extra methods. I have no idea what he meant by extra methods, but I guess somebody like Brody has to know more about that stuff than me.

I woke up at five in the morning after another night of tossing, turning, and imagining the worst possible scenarios, and decided to just give up on getting rest. Now, I'm standing in front of the door to Brody's room with two steaming coffees in my hands, contemplating how I'm going to knock, but it opens before I can.

The man stands in the doorway, looking sharp, and eyes me disapprovingly.

"You look like shit," he comments, grabbing the offered coffee.

"Yeah, whatever. Did you find anything new?" I sit down on his perfectly made bed and sigh after the first searing gulp of coffee goes down my throat.

"I did. I think I know where they are holding her," he replies calmly, and I almost drop the cup, spilling coffee on myself.

"What? Why the fuck aren't we already going, then? How did you find out?" I yell, ready to run in whatever direction he tells me.

"Calm down, Aidan. We need to be smart about it. Can't go guns blazing."

"Why not? That's what you did when your precious Jen was in danger, right? But since it's Claire, you don't give a fu-"

"Hey!" Brody booms, and my body straightens. His nostrils flare, and I take a step back when he comes to loom above me.

"Look, man. I get what you're going through. I do. But you need to pull yourself together. There are only two of us. And fuck knows how many of them. I already scoped the place, and I think there is a way for us to get there. However, you need to have your head in the game. This can't go wrong, or you'll lose her. You got me?"

"Yeah. Shit," I rub my face and sigh before sitting back down. "You already scoped the place? On your own? You could've woken me."

Brody smiles and takes a sip of his coffee before he leans on the chest of drawers, his legs crossing at the ankles. At that moment, it's not hard to imagine him doing this kind of police stuff every day. For a second, I wonder if it weren't for his leg getting so badly hurt that he'd be interested in returning to work in the law enforcement field again.

"Thought about waking your ass. Decided against it. And it was a good call, seeing your outburst just now."

"Probably," I admit dejectedly. "So, how did you find them?"

This time, it's Brody's turn to sigh tiredly. "I hit a breakthrough after you've gone to bed. Got excited, but then hit a brick wall. I had to admit we were running out of time here, so I had to call an old friend to help me out. Otherwise, I would still probably be running in circles here."

I give him a look. "A friend?"

"A hacker," Brody replies and scratches at his neck. "Someone I used to know during my time in the FBI. Actually, even before that. He's not exactly squeaky clean, and it cost a pretty penny for him to find what I was looking for. Anyway, I've got the address, and I'm pretty sure it's the place."

"How much money are we talking about?" I ask slowly, and by the way, he doesn't meet my eyes anymore. I know it had to be a-fucking-lot.

"Don't worry about it," he waves his big paw, but I'm already shaking my head stubbornly.

"Tell me."

He winces and then grumbles, "Thirty grand."

"Thirty grand? What the fuck?" I splutter.

"Yeah, he saw through my bluff and knew I was desperate. But it's done. It's over. Now we have to go get your girl and be out of this godforsaken place. I fucking hate Chicago."

I'm stumped, but I agree that if it was the only way, then it's definitely worth it. "Shit, man. I'll pay you back. I'll take a loan, I-"

"No need. You'll just have to work for me until you die," he jokes, but I don't find it funny.

"How did you get such an amount of cash on such short notice?"

"Oh, uh." Brody scratches his head again. "I already had it. I pulled it from our savings account we planned to use to finish the house with."

"What? Won't Jenny be angry with you?"

He gives me a patronizing look and shakes his head as if he thinks I am a complete moron. Which I know I am.

"Jenny was the one that told me to do it. She and Claire are like sisters; for me, there's no scenario in which I want to see my woman grieve because she lost her. For me personally, it wasn't exactly a hard decision either. It's just money. We're talking about the life of someone who's a part of our family."

"Do you..." I snap my mouth, finding it hard to voice the thoughts that have been swirling around my head ever since I found out someone grabbed her. "Do you think she's still alive?"

"I do." He says confidently, and I know it's just words, but I feel the heavy grip of fear letting go of my throat just a bit. "If they wanted her dead, she would be dead on the spot. That's what they supposedly did with the roommate. There has to be something they want from her if they decide to risk so much by kidnapping her in daylight and driving her all the way down here."

"But what do they want with her?" I ask, begging Brody with my eyes to make it all make sense.

He lets go of his cup and comes to slap me on the shoulder. "I'm sorry, brother, but I don't have an answer for that."

Once again, I feel the devastation over losing Claire before determination sets in. She's still out there somewhere. I can't act like a weeping pussy if I'm to rescue her. "Okay, so what now?"

"Now we go over the plan," is Brody's response before he opens his laptop.

CHAPTER XXIII

"I'M NOT SURE ABOUT this, man," I whisper to Brody, who squints at his phone, looking for something.

"You'll be fine," he mutters absentmindedly before exclaiming, "Got it!"

"What?"

"So here's the code to the gate. Remember, you need to go in and behave like this is exactly the place that you're supposed to be at. You can handle a gun, right?"

"Um, yeah, but I think you would be way more suitable for that than me. What if they know about me?"

"I doubt it, but it is a possibility. Anyway, you're better suited for the job, believe me. It has to be you. My leg makes me too distinguishable, and in no way would they allow an invalid dude working on the perimeter. Maybe they knew Claire was seeing someone or somehow learned about her past. However, I know men like the Ramirez brothers. They aren't concerned about people that they don't see as a threat. I doubt they even know their guards' names except those they allow close to them. Just wear a scowl on your face, which shouldn't be too hard when you think about whom the guards work for, and play a brainless mass of cells, which shouldn't be a problem for you either, right?"

"Fuck you, man," I snap, and Brody chuckles before shaking my shoulder lightly.

"You'll be fine, man. Just stick to the plan, don't let the emotions take over your actions, and you'll be dandy. Ready?"

"As I'll ever be," I sigh.

"Good, let's go grab your woman then, so you can show her that you're truly worthy of that second chance she gave you, yeah?"

"Yes, let's do this," I say, then pause before opening the door. "Hey, Brody."

He looks up from his phone once again and raises his brows expectantly.

I rub my sweaty palms on my suit pants and clear my throat nervously. "Um, just, thank you for everything. I owe you forever. Not just for what we're about to do now. I mean..."

"It's fine. We're cool. Now, before you go all sappy on me, you have a mission to do, soldier."

"Right."

I'm coming, baby. I just hope that it's not too late.

I move away from the car, trying to look casual and go around the corner to wait for the right time. When it's twelve o'clock, I cross the street in the direction of the white mansion half-hidden behind a tall fence and nicely trimmed hedges and confidently strut toward the back gate. The whole layout of the place is still vivid in my memory from the time Brody pulled it up on his laptop this morning.

I honestly don't know how he managed to gather so much info on such short notice, but I guess thirty grand will open some doors for a man.

Three guys dressed the same as me already stand there, chatting about yesterday's game, and I know the exact moment when they spot me because the conversation stops mid-sentence, and they all adopt a confrontational stance.

"Hey," I nod casually.

"Hey," the closest one to me replies. "You new here?"

"Nah, man. Just switchin' from the night shift." I say confidently, grateful for my time in prison for the first time since it taught me how to speak with guys who are trying to pick a fight.

"Droppin' in for Luke?" The man asks, and I know better than to answer directly. For all I know, Luke can be a made-up name.

"Don't know the name. The boss said to be here at noon, so here I am."

"Leave him be, Six," the shortest of the three says, shaking his head like he's fed up with his colleagues' territorial behavior.

"Come on then," the third guy says and makes a step toward the digital panel that will open the gate.

The first man, named Six, I guess, stops him with a hand to the chest, still looking suspicious. "No. Let the new guy do it."

I shrug, trying to look unbothered, but it's hard to contain the slight shake of my hand. I try to punch in the numbers provided to me by Brody as fast as possible before the other men notice.

There's a moment when the system lags, and my heart stops just for a fraction of a second. The vision of alarms blaring and bullets piercing my body enters my brain, but I soon relax when the small light above the panel turns green, and the door buzzes open.

I let them go first and then, as smoothly as possible, put the tape on the door mechanism just as Brody showed me, pretending that I have trouble closing the gate properly, and then come face to face with Six.

"Problem?"

"No, man. Just this fucking door always jammin'. Drives me fuckin' nuts," I say grumpily and move past him.

Please, don't go and check. Please, don't go and check.

The guy falls into step with me and looks more at ease.

"I told the boss there's a problem with that gate, but you know, Serg. Always has more important things to do than listen to his staff whining."

I hum in my throat and follow the pair going ahead. When we enter the house, I scan the place briefly, trying to look like I've seen it a thousand times before, and just as my companions march confidently through the corridors.

I must admit that the mansion's interior is impressive, and it's obvious the brothers don't suffer from lack of funds. The rooms we pass all look like they are straight from a house design magazine, but you can still see that someone actually lives here. It only further proves that Brody was right that this is the actual place where Sergio and Nico live if the giant fence and swarm of security guards weren't already a strong argument for that statement.

The brothers have three other, bigger mansions under their name, yet this one stood out among the others. First, it's not so in your face as the other buildings, and could just look like a house of people that enjoy their privacy. Secondly, it was officially bought by their cousin a year ago. However, the man himself is currently serving time in federal prison. And have been doing that for almost five years. So, it was a bit surprising to find that this was the only place that appeared to have a full staff on the payroll. Ramirez hired a cleaning company, and there are many bills proving that they ordered food and other 'services' here.

We know all of that from Brody's secret contact.

It pains me to think about the money because I would have to sell an organ to get that amount. If it weren't for Brody and Jenny, I'd be fucking useless in a situation like this. My bank account can attest to how poor I am.

But if the provided information checks out and helps me save Claire, then I don't care if it takes me my whole life to work for Brody as a literal slave to pay this debt as long as I find her safe and sound. As long as I have her with me.

I'm not sure what position I should take in the house, so I just let the other guys go to their designated spots and greet the other men who can leave their posts and go home.

I hope Brody had enough time to slip through the gate unnoticed. I wait for my phone to vibrate with a message, but it's staying annoyingly unmoving in my pocket.

He's supposed to message me when he gets in. Then, when he's ready for my move, and the third time, when he gets her. The plan is for me to create a distraction while he finds the basement, get Claire if she's actually there, and get her out before anyone finds out what happened.

Finally, the first message comes through, and I secretly peek at my phone.

I'm in. Sorry for the delay. Distract them so I can go in unnoticed.

I eye the two guys standing by the two large windows in the living room and then notice a third guy walking down the corridor.

Okay, what's the best way to distract them? I look into a room that looks like some kind of reading room and notice an open book on a desk and, right next to it, a pack of cigarettes with an ashtray. Bingo!

I check one more time to see if I'm alone and then walk into the room to grab a cigarette and look for a lighter to spark it up. Then I set the first pages of the book on fire and quickly stage everything so it looks like it was the cigarette that caused it. Maybe it's not the smartest idea, but I hope a fire going on in one of the rooms will allow Brody enough time to check the basement.

Just as I sneak out of there, the fire alarm starts blaring in the whole house, and I slip into a closed room two doors down when I hear footsteps and then some yelling, "Bring some fucking water in here!"

"What about the extinguisher?" A voice calls back.

"Fuck the extinguisher! You want to be the one to destroy the boss's precious books with that shit?"

My phone vibrates with a message.

Good job. Wait for me upstairs, close to the exit.

I stick my head back into the corridor and see the group of men gathered by the reading room, all looking displeased but, to my relief, paying no mind to anything else.

My steps are slow and measured as I back away from the corridor, but my phone vibrates again.

We've got a problem. Come downstairs NOW.

I change directions and slip onto the staircase with my heart in my throat. Something must've gone wrong. That wasn't the plan.

My shoes squeak loudly on the steps, and I cringe, but when nothing happens for ten seconds, I continue down the stairs. I go quickly through the labyrinth of corridors, trying every door I pass until I spot the open one. Dimmed light coming from it, as well as sounds of someone struggling with something.

I get in, and the image of what I find there will surely be imprinted in my memory, only to become a visitor in my darkest, most terrifying nightmares for years to come.

Brody kneels over Claire's lifeless, pale body, his hands posed on her chest as he presses it to the rhythm and counts quietly.

I stand there like hypnotized, my brain unable to process the thought of what's taking place until Brody notices me.

"Fuck, man. They'll be coming soon. Do you know how to do CPR?"

"N-no." I stammer, unashamed by the tears blurring my vision. "C-Claire. What?"

I make a step further into the room and right away stop, unable to come any closer.

Brody continues to press on her chest, only pausing to extract his gun from the back of his pants, and passes it to me. It slides on the floor and lands at my feet.

"This is my gun. It's registered in my name. Whatever you do, don't leave prints on it, you hear me?"

"I..." I frown at him, not knowing what he means. What does he want me to do?

"I already called for help. The ambulance and the police are on their way. Hopefully, they're going to be here before the goons come running, but if not, you need to shoot anyone who gets close. Don't kill them. Just immobilize or something. And whatever you do. Don't leave your fingerprints on the gun."

I have trouble following his words, my eyes going back to Claire's pale face, and I gulp.

"Aidan!" Brody roars. "Get it together. She will make it. I promise. But you need to watch my back."

Blinking furiously, I take off my suit jacket and rip it apart from the sleeve with strength I didn't even know I possessed before I pick up the gun with the piece of fabric. It's not ideal, but it will have to do.

I hear Brody say, "We've got a pulse!" Just as one of the men in the dark corridor notices me standing there.

"Hey, man! What are you doin' here? It turned out we've got a breach..." he stops when he sees the gun pointed at him, and immediately, his hand goes to the holster on his hip.

"Don't move!" I command. "Let us out of here, and nothing bad will happen."

The man snorts and makes a move to get his gun. He stops half-motion when an earsplitting bang echoes through the basement and then glances at the red, growing stain on his stomach. He puts both hands to stop the bleeding before swaying on his feet and falling to the ground.

The acidic taste of vomit hits my throat, but all I can focus on is Brody, who's now lifting Claire from the floor. She's so small that she looks like a child in his embrace. One of her arms swings down, and I notice the little syringe still stuck in there.

My heart breaks even more. I gently grab her arm and remove the needle before I move my hand to grab her cold palm and kiss it.

"You're going to be okay," I whisper, though now those words feel painfully empty.

The sounds of sirens reach us from outside, causing Brody and I to snap our heads up.

"Okay. You did great, kid. Now take her, and I'll handle those fuckers."

I take Claire from him and tuck her to my chest after Brody retrieves the gun from my hand.

"I think I killed the guy," I whisper shakily.

"Don't worry about it," Brody says, though I can see the deep lines of worry stretch on his forehead. "All that matters is getting us out of here and taking Claire to a hospital."

I nod my head and follow him out. We're not even two steps into the corridor when three uniformed men appear, weapons in hand.

"Chicago PD! Drop the weapon. Let go of the girl!"

Brody lifts his hands before slowly lowering the one that holds his gun. His posture is composed, even though he wobbles slightly on his injured leg as he moves to kneel. He allows the cops to cuff him up and blinks at me calmly.

I see one of the cops attending to the guard bleeding out on the floor and speaking to the radio attached to his shoulder for medics to send another gurney downstairs.

"Sir, I need you to let off the girl and get on the ground," a cop closest to me barks, but all I can do is squeeze Claire's body to me, scared out of my mind. What if this is the last time that I get to hold her?

"Do as the man says, Aidan. We're going to straighten it all out while the medics help her, okay?" Brody's voice is soft.

"Okay," I whisper and drop a quick kiss to Claire's temple before I lie her down.

As the cop presses me down and cuffs me, a group of paramedics arrives, one pair going straight for Claire.

"What happened?" The young doctor asks, looking around to find someone who will answer him, already opening his medical bag.

"She..." my voice is gruff, so I clear my throat. "I think she overdosed."

"What did she take?"

"I, uh... No idea. The syringe is still in the room. I don't know what was in it."

"Alright. We're going to take care of her," I'm informed as the man waves for the other paramedic to bring the gurney before they strap her in.

I know there are more things happening around me like the cops telling me my rights. Brody says something to me about staying quiet until he can make some calls and everything straightens out. I know the bodyguard I shot is being attended to, and the doctors keep yelling something at each other.

But it feels miles away from me. All I see is Claire being wheeled away, a mask put on her beautiful face before she disappears from my life once again.

I want to weep and pray to God that she'll be fine. I don't even care that after breaking the parole and shooting a man, I will probably never see the daylight outside of bars ever again. I don't care as long as she makes it.

I know how insufferable my world was without her in it. I can't go through it.

I'm being dragged up violently before the cop pushes me further through the house until we come to the big, open, two-story living room. There's more police just coming in, arresting people left and right. I notice a young FBI agent walk in and nod at Brody in a way so subtle that I wonder if I didn't imagine it. A forensics crew comes in after him, and they start to tear the place down right away.

I'm being lined up next to the other men, and I see the one named Six throwing me a murderous glare. But I'm numb. Observing the things happening in front of me as if I were watching a movie play out.

One of the forensics comes out from the room to my left with a bag of white powder and waves the others to join him.

The brothers are not here, but I imagine that this will be the beginning of their downfall. I'm sure I have Brody to thank for that. And it doesn't matter what they go down for; I will go down along with them as long as Claire is free and safe.

CHAPTER XXIV

IT'S BEEN FIVE DAYS since I've been put in a small cell. The police officers are unwilling or unable to tell me shit, and I'm literally on the verge of losing my mind.

I have no idea what's been going on outside these walls, and it's fucking hell. After the first night spent in the arrest, I got permission to make my one phone call, and I used it to call Jenny, of all people. Of course, she already knew everything from Brody, who's apparently been out of the police station after just a few hours of interrogation. She also told me that Claire still hadn't woken up but was stable.

But that was four days ago. And not a word.

"Linden, you're out of here!" I hear coming from the end of the room. I'm so stiff and numb that I don't react at first. "You deaf? Stand up. You're getting out. There's someone waiting for you." The police officer grumbles and unlocks the cell.

My tired brain catches up eventually, and I get up from the cot to walk out on leaden legs.

I go through the motions on autopilot, too tired and sleep-deprived to actually comprehend what the officers are saying, and just nod when it looks like I was asked a question.

The sun blinds me as I walk out of the precinct. I take a deep breath and march forward. Then, I notice someone waving at me.

I was sure to see Brody waiting for me, so the sight of Sandra leaning on her black BMW throws me off for a bit even more when I notice how normal and humane she appears today.

There's no bright red lipstick coloring her mouth or actually any kind of makeup. Her hair is down and swaying slowly in the wind. The lack of high heels makes her look ridiculously smaller than usual. The sweatshirt and yoga pants she wears look expensive and new, but it's still weird, a weird contrast to her usual sexy outfits.

"Here's the little culprit," she announces as a way of greeting me and surprises me with a quick hug.

I know I smell like shit, but Sandra doesn't seem to mind. She moves back to give me a critical once over, for the first time bringing a worried mother to my mind, before she slaps me on the chest.

"That was really stupid what you did, Aidan. Do you have any idea just how much paperwork your little trip to Chicago landed on my desk? You owe me big time. As does Damon, actually."

"Um, Sandra? Not that it's not nice to see a familiar face after the week I had, but... What are you doing here?"

Then, a thought hits me, and I step back from her.

"Did you come here to transport me back to prison? Because I broke the parole and um... shot the-"

"La-la-la-la," she sticks fingers in her ears and exclaims, "Didn't hear that."

I snap my mouth shut and give her a questioning look, to which she rolls her eyes.

"Come on, jailbird. I'm here to give you a ride home. Brody is unavailable because his lady love is giving birth to their offspring as we speak. I'm so jealous..." She opens the door to her car and motions for me to get in. "Anyway, we'll talk on the way."

"Jenny is in labor?" I question as soon as I'm inside the car, and Sandra peels off from the police parking lot.

"Yeah. The timing isn't the greatest, but that's life, right?" She says it in a normal tone, not her usual flirty, breathy one, and I give her a sideways glance.

"Sandra, is everything okay?"

"Hmm?" She checks the side mirror before joining the traffic. "I'm fine, Aidan. Just some personal shit I have to deal with. But that's not why we're here, right? From what I've heard, you've been busy breaking parole left and right."

"So, what happens now? Will you drive me back to prison right away, or do I wait for a judge..." I stop mid-sentence when Sandra starts laughing.

"Drive you back to prison? No way! Why would I ever do that? You're a good guy, Aidan. I'm so jealous of Claire, to be honest. Well, maybe not with the... you know, the things that happened. But to have a man set aside his future and risk his life to get her back, no matter the consequences? Oh my God, that is a dream come true. An amazing love story."

She tries to sound like her usual self, but I still detect the pain in her voice when she says it, and for the first time, I actually wonder what makes a person like Sandra the way she is. I always thought she was a crazy nymphomaniac whose kink is fucking criminals. Now, as she's sitting next to me, underdressed, I realize that it's probably just an armor she puts on for whatever reason.

"Anyway, the way I see it is you got my permission to leave the state and went to look for your girlfriend who went missing. Then you found her, and the men who were holding her hostage attacked you. Brody shot one of the guards in self-defense, and that's the end of the story. The rest was dealt with by the police, and now you're free to go. I'm just here to give you a ride."

"But Brody didn't shoot him. I did," I argue.

"What did you say? I don't think I heard you properly..." Sandra puts a hand to her ear. "Did you just say he did shoot the guy? Yep. That's right. He did, and it's fine. He won't be prosecuted for that. And neither will you. Your parole officer took care of that." She sends me a wink and concentrates back on the road.

For a moment, I'm speechless. "Why would you do that for me?"

"Because it's the right thing to do. And because I like to see people get their happily ever after. You're not the bad guy here, Aidan. Believe me, I encountered plenty of those. And I could never forgive myself if I was the one turning you into one."

"Wow. Thank you." I mutter, perplexed. And then have to ask, "Do you know how's Claire doing?"

"Sorry, but no." She glances at me and sees my frown. "I'm sure she's fine, Aidan. She has to be, right? After the shit you went through, she has to be. Your story needs to have a happy ending now. I refuse to believe otherwise."

Sandra concentrates back on the road, and I concentrate on the view out the window. God, I hope she's right. As I watch us turning on an interstate, my eyelids get heavier and heavier, and before I know it, I doze off.

THE NEXT DAY, I GET a text from Brody stating that they are back home and to stop by.

I have no idea what it means and if that implies that Claire is back home too, but I'm already on my feet and leaving my apartment before I even finish reading the message.

It's not even fifteen minutes later when I knock at their door and wait impatiently. To my surprise, it's Brody's aunt Ruth who opens the door, the kid, Henry, closely behind her.

"Oh, hi!" I exclaim way too loudly and immediately lower my voice. "Um, Brody said to come?"

"Hi, Aidan," the woman greets me warmly and envelops me in a hug. It's the second woman giving me a motherly hug in two days, and I have to admit I don't exactly hate it. "I'm glad to see you safe and sound."

Still, I quickly step back and look around, searching the place, and right away notice that something is different. It takes me a second to understand what is amiss apart from the person herself. Her things. All gone.

I don't know what my face showed, but Ruth steps into my line of sight.

"She's fine, boy. Claire is going to be alright," her voice is soft, and the smile is in place, but I take notice of the unspoken sadness in her eyes, too.

"Where is she?" I choke out and lift my head when I hear footsteps.

Brody comes down the stairs, looking just as bad as I feel, with dark circles under his tired eyes. His hair is a mess, and his shirt is wrinkled, but there's one thing that shines through the image, and it's the smile of an accomplished man with a great family life.

Something that I doubt that I will ever feel on my own face.

His happy expression fades a bit when he notices me, and he tells his aunt to take Henry and leave us to talk.

"How's Jenny? And the baby?" I ask when I have enough of him staring at me with pity in the now silent room.

"Jen did spectacular. She's sleeping with the baby upstairs. We have a healthy girl. Her name is Layla." The pride shines in his eyes, and I wish I could be more expressive when it comes to how happy I am for them because I am.

"That's great. Congrats," I say thickly, and my fists clench at my sides.

"Aidan, Claire went into rehab," he announces like we are talking about the weather, and I stare at him.

The confusion is instant. "Rehab? Why?"

"I don't know, man. That was her decision after she woke up in the hospital. Of course, we respected her wishes and drove her to a facility she chose."

"Where is it? Can I contact her?" I step closer, eager to hear her voice to make sure that she's actually safe.

"No, I'm sorry. She specifically asked us not to tell you," he declares, looking awkward.

"What?" My heart breaks, as well as my voice.

"Yeah..." he rubs his chin between his fingers and then seems to remember something. "Oh, she asked me to give you this."

He walks to the small desk in the corner and takes out a small white envelope from the top drawer before handing it to me.

The simple, almost child-like handwriting on the top has my name on it, and I have to blink rapidly to get rid of the tears. I open it and read.

Aidan, I'm so sorry for leaving. I heard what you did and how you risked your life to get me away from that basement. I don't think there are words to express how much I love you and how much the thoughts about you helped me down there.

But there is something I must do for us now, too. I'm willing to fight the obstacles, too. Ready to fight my demons to ensure our future is safe.

Please, don't give up on us.

Love always, Claire.

"Are you okay, man?" Brody asks me tentatively after I've been staring at the paper for too long and rereading every word four times.

She didn't leave me. At least not permanently if I can trust the words in front of my eyes.

We're going to be fine. I have to believe that, and I have to give her the time to heal properly.

I collect myself and carefully fold the piece of paper to hide it in my pocket before I face Brody. He eyes me like I'm a wounded animal, and he's unsure whether I will pounce or freak out on him.

His face is almost shocked when I smile and say, "Yeah, man. I'm okay. We're going to be okay."

CHAPTER XXV

TWO MONTHS LATER

A groan passes from my lips as I lift another wooden beam along with Tommy before passing it to the waiting arms above us.

Brody was adamant about finishing each ongoing project before the winter so he could then take some time off to be more at home with Jenny and the kids. So, for the last month, all we've been doing was taking double shifts and working on the rooftops.

When we're back in the evening, all I want to do is throw myself face down on the bed and sleep, just like my annoying roommate does. What I do instead is log into my online classes and study until I pass out from exhaustion.

I still haven't heard from Claire, and it's starting to weigh on me, too, but it's easier not to think about how much I miss her when I'm crushed by the amount of work I have.

Trying to keep the workflow going, Tommy and I bend to grab another beam when the voice of our new woodworker, Derek, sounds from above. "Yo! Who's that chick?"

One of the helpers, Pete, walks to the hole in the wall that will soon become a window and whistles loudly.

Brody comes to see what's the commotion about and steps next to him just as Tommy motions for me to continue. When we're on the job, there's nothing in this world that will distract my best friend.

"Holy shit! Look at those legs; I can already imagine them wrapped around my-" A slap echoes in the space, and we stop what we're doing. Pete massages the back of his head and scowls at Brody. "Ow! What the hell, boss?"

"Aidan! You're done for the day," the man says suddenly, still looking at the helper with disapproval, and I drop the heavy piece of wood.

"What? I didn't even fucking say anything," I complain. "Why the fuck are you punishing me for?"

"Not punishing. Rewarding," Brody says with a smirk before he limps away to throw over his shoulder, "Go outside."

Okay? I don't know what's this about, but if the guys are considering pranking me again, then I'm going to beat their asses. Well, maybe not my boss's, but the rest will surely regret fucking with me again.

I remove my gloves, throw them by the little bench where I left my jacket, and walk out of the building.

Cold wind hits me in the chest, and I shiver slightly. Just as predicted, there's nothing out there, and I curse loudly, ready to come back, when the sweetest fucking voice stops me.

"Damn, you're so hot when you're angry."

I almost break my neck with the speed my head whips to the side, and then watch with wide eyes as Claire steps from the shadows, big smile in place.

She's wearing a cute pink hat and a black coat that ends right above a skirt that reaches her mid-thigh. Her legs are covered with black tights and look extra long because of the high-heeled boots she has on.

I was never a man who paid much attention to the way women dress, but damn, right now, Claire looks like straight from a magazine, and it turns my blood into fire.

Her face looks slightly fuller, and her cheeks start to redden under my stare.

"Aidan? Are you still in there?" She giggles and walks closer.

My hands start shaking, my body begging me to touch her, but I press my palms to my sides, unable to fathom that she's really here, standing in front of me. My girl. Alive and healthy.

Her eyes go over my face slowly, and her smile turns soft like she understands that I need the moment to go over the onslaught of emotions.

"I missed you," she says. "Did you miss me?"

Stiffly, my head moves up and down, but I'm still not talking. Claire takes another tentative step forward.

"Just kiss her already!" A voice calls from above us, and I realize we've got an audience. Yet, there's nothing that could rip my eyes off the beautiful woman standing in front of me right now.

There could be an earthquake, and I wouldn't even care.

"You heard the man. Just kiss me already," Claire demands and something finally snaps in me.

I grab her by the hips and slam my lips to hers. She's ready for it and returns the kiss with just as much passion and impatience.

The catcalls from the other men barely register as I slam her back into the newly built wall, making the construction shake.

Claire's leg lifts to my hip, and I help her wrap around my hips as we continue to make out. My lips go to her neck, and she moans before the sound of someone clearing their throat somewhere close stops me from going further.

Tommy stands close by, his face tomato red, and I almost laugh at how uncomfortable the view of us two making out made him.

He lifts the keys to the apartment and once again clears his throat. "I, uh, you left this. I'm gonna... I'm gonna stay at Derek's tonight, so you can... spend time together?" With each word, he looks more and more mortified, and it takes everything in me not to call him out for it.

Slowly, I step away from the wall and allow Claire's legs to hit the ground before I grab the keys from his hand.

"Thanks, man," I grin happily.

Claire fixes her hair under the hat and lifts her hand in a small wave, "Hiya, Tommy!"

"Hi, Claire. It's nice to see you, so..." he looks anywhere but her and then steps away. "Anyway, have fun, you two,"

And then he's gone.

Claire and I look at each other knowingly before we run toward my truck. We both cackle like fools as I start the engine and back out the vehicle.

I'm barely catching my breath when I glance at Claire, and a new fit of laughter chokes me.

Man, I'm so fucking happy. I never knew it was possible.

THE DAY IS ALMOST OVER when we're both lying on my bed, worn out after showing each other who missed whom more. The open box of half-eaten large pizza we ordered placed next to the bed.

Claire is now only wearing her simple black underwear as she leans her back on the headboard with her legs stretched out. My head is on her thigh as I eye her lovingly, and honestly, I wish we could just stay like this for the whole eternity.

Her hand goes through my hair, the nails scraping my scalp slowly, making my body relax even more.

"Tell me about the rehab," I say gently, and Claire stops her movements for a moment before resuming, and I close my eyes.

"Honestly, it wasn't bad," she says softly. "Everyone was nice and set to help me get through it. The first week was the worst, obviously because my system craved whatever was in that syringe. But with each day, the need to get high lessened, and then something else took its place."

"What was it?" I ask carefully, my eyes opening to read her expression.

"The need to see you and be with you. The way I missed Jenny and the family that I became a part of. I was surprised to find that pull was way stronger than the one toward drugs ever was. Did it feel good to pump my body with that shit? Yes, I'm never going to lie about that. But did it come close to how you make me feel?" She shakes her head and moves her body lower so our foreheads touch. "Not even close, Aidan. Nothing compares."

"I love you," I say gruffly, and don't hide my eyes when they become teary. I will never hide my feelings in front of this magical woman. She possesses all of me. There's no part of me that is not already hers, even my tears.

"I love you," she says and kisses me slowly.

"You think we can do this?" I hear myself muttering sleepily.

"I think we can do everything. As long as it's together," she whispers, and we both fall asleep.

EPILOGUE

It's early spring as we stand in my friends' garden, and I sip at the alcohol-free beer that tastes exactly how it sounds.

I eye the enthusiastic faces around before stopping on Nora, who's currently playing tag with Amelia's daughters and Henry. They've been a foster family for her for a while now, and I know Amelia and her husband, Mark, are seriously thinking of adopting her. It's clear that they absolutely adore her.

And it makes me happy to see Nora smile so freely. I know the pain is still there, but it's absolutely fascinating how the right people can take even the biggest hurt in your life off your shoulders and carry you through each day.

I should know something about it.

My eyes search for Aidan, and I find him in a heated conversation with Brody as they both glance toward Jenny. They quickly exchange something, and the big man limps away before I take his place.

"What was that about?" I ask worriedly, but to my surprise, Aidan grins in response.

His eyes lift above my head, and he grabs my shoulders to turn me around.

"Just look," he says under his breath.

The music stops suddenly, and I swing my attention toward the table to see what's going on. Aunt Ruth shushes her husband with a jab when he continues to laugh at something one of the men at the table said, and then I see what got everyone's attention.

Brody kneels in front of an oblivious Jenny as she coos into the little baby carriage with their baby girl and then lifts her head when it gets awfully quiet.

"What got you all so spooked," she throws, and then finally notices Brody at her feet.

"Did you fall again? What did I tell you about trying to walk without the stick?" She grumbles but then frowns when he chuckles, his face getting slightly pink when she mentions his inability to walk without the aid.

"Actually, this fall was premeditated, Sweetheart," he takes out a small black box out of his pocket and glances at her with a face full of love, anticipation, and fear. All the women around gasp, including Jenny, and her eyes immediately fill with tears.

"Jen, you are the embodiment of a perfect woman for me. The moment I fell for you, I fell hard and was adamant about not letting you go. You are my true love, my friend, my partner in crime, and the mother of my children. I know we've talked about it, and with everything..." he blinks a few times and takes a deep breath. "But I want it all. I want you to be my wife for better or for worse. I want to claim in front of the whole world that you are mine. I want to-"

At that moment, Jenny drops to her knees and kisses Brody straight on the mouth without any care that we're all watching. Just when it starts to feel a bit uncomfortable, and I'm about to look away, she leans back with a happy laugh.

"What took you so long, Handsome?"

"Is that a yes?" He asks slowly.

"It's an "of course I'll fucking marry you" yes," she exclaims throwing her arms around him as everyone starts cheering.

They both stand up from their kneeling position before he presents her with a simple yet pretty ring and puts it on her finger with shaking hands.

Then Brody grabs her hand and pulls it up to yell, "She said yes!"

My own happy tears blur my sight, and I glance to the side at a proud-looking Aidan as he claps while watching the happy couple in front of us.

"Did you know he was planning this? You don't look that surprised," I accuse him playfully.

Aidan twists his head to look at me, his face softening like always when his eyes land on me.

"Yeah, dude was a bundle of nerves ever since he decided to pop the question. He was insufferable. I'm glad she said yes because I can't imagine what would happen to him and us, his poor workers, otherwise."

We go to congratulate the happy couple on their engagement. And soon, what was meant to be a little backyard gathering with friends and family turns into a real party with champagne and a makeshift dance floor on the grass.

My back is sweaty, and my hair glues itself to my forehead from how long we've been dancing, and I'm glad when the music switches to something slower. Aidan brings me closer to his body and sways us slowly before we make a small twirl.

"Do you think that could ever be us?" He asks quietly, only for me to hear. I glance behind us at Jenny and Brody, laughing together at something Henry said before they all hug.

"You mean, like marriage and kids?" He nods, and I take a moment to think before I can reply honestly.

"Eventually, probably yes. I would want that. But is that going to be a given in my future? In our future? I don't know Aidan. It's still too much... to think about big steps like that." I frown at him. "Is that going to be an issue for you? If I want to wait?"

Aidan grabs my hand to kiss it and starts swaying again without his eyes leaving mine.

"Claire, I love you. Everything about you. The good, the not-so-good, and the little bit crazy... I love you in every way possible. Married, unmarried, with children or no children. And as long as you're mine, and as long as I can make you happy, I won't be needing anything else. You always come first. I'll wait."

Oh. Wow. I think my heart might explode from the overload of love and sappy feelings that his words evoke.

I tilt my head up and give him a small kiss.

"You do," I mutter against his lips, and he gives me a questioning look. "You do make me happy."

I glance to the side to check what everyone else is doing before a mischievous smile overtakes my mouth. "Actually, I have a little idea about what you could do right now to make me even more happy, Mr. Linden."

"Ms. Thompson, what kind of naughty thoughts are running around in that pretty head of yours," he says in a lower voice. The desire is burning in his eyes.

"I could tell you..." I say and bite my lip before going to his ear and whispering. "Or I can show you."

I can hear his hard breath intake, and after checking one last time, if no one pays us any mind, I drag him to the other side of the house.

When we're around the corner, we both start to laugh like teenagers, eager to do something naughty, but then stop short when we see a young woman, or more like a teenage girl, standing in the driveway, looking around with an angry look on her face.

"Who's that?" Aidan asks quietly.

"No idea," I throw and move forward with my hand enveloped in his. The girl finally notices me, and her face quickly transforms from furious and wrong to a sweet and pleasant one. Too quickly. Maybe a normal person wouldn't see it, but I recognize the act instantly, and I'm all of a sudden on edge.

"Hi, may I help you?" I ask with a sweet smile and eye her. Something about her sparks my mind, but I can't really put my finger on it. She looks familiar.

"Oh, hi. Um, sorry if I'm trespassing. I'm actually looking for someone. Do you live here?"

"I do," I say, even though that's not entirely true since I've been staying at Aidan's more than not lately. "Who is it that you're looking for?"

She glances at the house and then says. "I'm looking for a woman named Jennifer Wallace. Does she live here? Or maybe you know her?"

I don't like the way she says Jenny's name, and I glance at Aidan quickly to check if he heard that, too. His lifted eyebrows show me that, indeed, there's something off here.

He squeezes my hand before lifting his chin at her. "Say we know her. Who's asking?"

The girl steps from foot to foot and licks her lips. "My name is Molly Barnett..."

Okay... Why does that last name sound familiar?

"And apparently, I'm Jennifer's half-sister..."

My eyes open wide, and I throw "Oh shit" the same time Aidan says. "Oh fuck no."

And then we all jump as if we were just caught doing something bad when a voice reaches us from behind.

"Claire? Are you guys here? I need you to..." Jenny rounds the corner of the house and stops short before her mouth opens and closes like she's a fish thrown out of the ocean trying to find water.

Instant recognition enters her gaze as her face turns pale. "Oh fuck no."

"That's what I said," Aidan mumbles, and I glare at him.

The sister steps around us and slowly peruses Jenny with coldness in her eyes.

"You clearly know who I am. Which isn't surprising since you're responsible for ruining my life," she growls before charging at my best friend.

"Oh fuck no," I hear myself whispering before I rush to the rescue.

I think our unusual family just got bigger by adding a new troubled member.

THE END

Thank you for taking the time to read Claire's story!
If you enjoyed the journey, I would be incredibly grateful for your feedback. Please consider leaving a review or rating the book on a chosen platform.
If you are interested in any future releases and promotions, please visit me at https://www.hannahmartinezauthor.com and sign up for my newsletter to ensure that you are always up-to-date.